About the author

Anita Loos was born in California in 1888, where she was a child stage actress, and later wrote movie scripts. *The New York Hat* (1912), starring Mary Pickford and Lionel Barrymore, catapulted Loos to Hollywood fame. Her prolific pen supplied scenarios for among others D W Griffith, Douglas Fairbanks, Spencer Tracy and Clark Gable. Her script for *Red Headed Woman* (1932) revived Jean Harlow's career. Her best-selling novels *Gentlemen Prefer Blondes* (1925) and its sequel *But Gentleman Marry Brunettes* (1928) sold several million copies and drew rave comments from such diverse readers as Winston Churchill, James Joyce, Edith Wharton and H L Mencken. By the 1930s she was working for $1000 a week at MGM and living in Beverly Hills. She also wrote works for the stage including *Happy Birthday* and adaptations of Colette's *Gigi* and *Cheri*. She published two further novels *A Mouse is Born* (1950) and *No Mother to Guide Her* (1960) and two volumes of autobiography, *A Girl Like I* (1966) and *Kiss Hollywood Good-by* (1969). She was still working on new projects when she died of a heart attack in 1981.

No Mother to Guide Her

PRION HUMOUR CLASSICS

* for copyright reasons these titles are not available in the USA or Canada in the Prion edition.

No Mother To Guide Her

ANITA LOOS

with a new introduction by
KATHY LETTE

PRION

This edition published in 2000 by
Prion Books Limited, Imperial Works,
Perren Street, London NW5 3ED

ISBN 1-85375-366-1

Jacket design by Jon Gray
Jacket image courtesy of Hulton Getty

Printed and bound in Great Britain
by Creative Print & Design, Wales

To Lansing Marshall—
wherever he is—
and to Gladys,
who went through the siege
of Hollywood with us

INTRODUCTION

by KATHY LETTE

Anita Loos is a name which should be on the tip of every tongue (which is, after all, a girl's favourite place to be). This re-issue of *No Mother to Guide Her* (reworked as a novel by Loos in 1960 having first appeared as a serial in *Cosmopolitan* in 1930 under the title *The Better Things in Life*) is a reminder that the bonsai brunette who wrote *Gentlemen Prefer Blondes* penned much more than that one comic mistresspiece.

Loos wrote four novels, two musicals (adapting Collette's novel for *Gigi*), four stage plays and no less than 165 screenplays—most notably *The Women* (a cinematic tour de farce which should bear a danger sign reading 'Warning. Extremely Hormonal Females for Next Kilometre'). This was a woman who obtained her first screen credit (from D W Griffiths, no less) when she was still a teenager. It read: 'Macbeth, by William Shakespeare and Anita Loos'.

Of all her satirical creations, *Gentlemen Prefer Blondes* remains her best known work. Loos admitted that the novel was inspired by H L Mencken's flirtation with a 'stupid little blonde'. 'My only purpose,' Loos wrote in one of her four autobiographies, 'was to make Henry laugh at himself.' And an entire nation laughed with him, at this send up of the cream of society and how it curdles. Her shrewd account of the 1920s sex war begins with Lorelei's acquittal on a charge of attempted murder. Liberated, she's off to New York, now sniffing for trouser and taking no prisoners. Because the law of the jungle dictates that you always hunt in pairs, Lorelei teams up with Dorothy and they set out on high-heeled safari. Their prey? Anything tall, dark and bankable. (These gals were equipped with everything bar a net and a tranquilliser gun). The moneyed bachelors of the time needed an Anti-Husband Hunting League for their own protection. In Lorelei, men with money to burn had truly met their match. (Well, if God hadn't meant them to hunt men, he wouldn't have created suspender belts, right?)

Power comes to her female characters when they pretend not to have any. By impersonating airheads they become heiresses. In truth, it actually takes a lot of intelligence to look that stupid. Their scheming ways (Lorelei had an eye-lash batting average to rival Joe DiMaggio) seem monstrously manipulative today. But it's important to remember the moral hypocrisy and misogyny of the 1920s—in the battle between the sexes the men had all the weapons. Women were denied political representation on the principle declared by one Southern congressman that giving the vote to women would 'disrupt the family, which is the unit of society and when you disrupt the family, you destroy the home, which is the foundation stone of the Republic'. Women also lacked equal access to education, the trades and professions. They were expected to pluck their eyebrows, not their highbrows. Law Schools remained closed to them (Harvard did not admit women until the 1950s)—and social stereotyping was endemic. With no vote and no contraception, what options were available?

Apart from mind-numbing factory work, governessing or domestic service, it was prostitution or marriage (often a tautology in those days).

Anita Loos' protagonists provided an antidote to all the wet and wimpy female fictional characters prevalent in fiction at the time. Lorelei was the Madonna of her day, flouting tradition and challenging hypocritical sexual mores. (And what a survivor! After the nuclear holocaust, all that'll be left are a couple of cockroaches —and Lorelei). Okay, she had a few minor faults: snobbery and sexual kleptomania (Lorelei climbed the social ladder—lad by lad); and husband-hunting (she wasn't interested in Mr Right, but Lord, Sir, Marquis Right at the very least). But what makes Loos' female characters so radical and anarchic is the fact they are not 'fallen women'. Fall? Good God no. They leapt, no, bungee-jumped into debauchery. Their domesticity was limited to the sewing of wild oats, and as for home cooking—you know, that place where a husband thinks his wife is—the only bucket Lorelei ever encountered was the one with the champagne in it.

These were schizophrenic times for women—the era of suffragettes and showgirls. Through her film scripts and fiction, Loos fashioned the image of the 'flapper'— the liberated, one-liner-laden girl-about-town; the sort of woman who'd been on more laps than a napkin. *Redheaded Woman* caused a hurricane of protest in 1932 because her protagonist (played by Jean Harlow) never pays for her sins. She ends up having her cake and eating it…and not putting on any weight either. (In Anita-Loos-Land, the best way to get rid of 'unsightly fat' is to divorce that couch-potato hubby).

11

Ironically, for all her warnings about 'gold diggers', Loos herself was a misfortune hunter, who found her Mr Wrong. Her marriage to John Emerson 20 years or so her senior was a disaster. He demanded writing co-credits, cheated on her, took all her money (granting her a paltry allowance) and lost it in bad financial investments, and even tried to strangle her, before he was diagnosed as a schizophrenic. Despite all this, Anita Loos continued to worship the water she thought he walked on.

Although the heroines in Loos' books and films appear to have the brain frequency of house plants, they are actually sharp and shrewd; adept at that most virtuosic gymnastic feat of keeping a man at arm's length whilst never losing her grip on him. No, her cruellest barbs are reserved for men. Most are rich with money and poor with personality. In *Gentlemen Prefer Blondes*, Henry Spoffard uses his personality as a contraceptive, while in *No Mother to Guide Her* Elmer Bliss (an evangelical newspaper columnist) is the kind of man who sends his shirt out to be stuffed. Her movie mogul, Mr. Goldmark, represents another of her favourite satirical targets—the self-made man who worships his creator. (The boy who pulled wings off flies at school often turns into the man who adds wings onto mansions as an adult).

In this novel, Loos combines three of her favourite targets—male gullibility, the double standards of the moral crusaders, and the ridiculousness of Hollywood. Despite Viola Lake's wholesome screen image, this is a woman for whom the word 'commit' can only be used next to the word 'murder'. The notorious Barco murder case threatens to blow the lid off the film colony and make public Viola's diaries in the process. Enter the moral crusader Elmer Bliss (the type who thinks 'mutual orgasm' is an insurance company) who aims to become her Knight in Shining Armour…but soon takes to the good life like champagne off a duck's back.

In chapters tongue-in-cheekily entitled 'The Brighter Side of Murder' and 'Could Hollywood be Heaven?' Loos satirises an American epoch, its psychological sweet-tooth (the craving for sentimentality) disguising the bitter after-taste of the orgies attended in the desperate 'pursuit of happiness'. The book's sardonic, caustic wit is drier than an AA clinic, and its satirical themes are still topical: nepotism, cults, sex scandals, pill-popping, multiple divorce (getting richer by decrees) and the Mexico gulf between beliefs and behaviour. Loos is most savage about the self-righteous, the smug, the sanctimonious—all those who feign respectability while policing other people's morals.

Notwithstanding the advent of the Women's Movement, contemporary movies offer vocational guidance in bimbofication. Think about it. Apart from the odd Pretty Woman prostitute or Fatal Attraction psychopath, what role models do we girls have? Sharon Stone flashing her fallopians? The flibbertigibbet (played by Kim Basinger or Demi Moore) whose sole concern is on what side her bed is buttered? It appears to be a Hollywood rule that any female character with a witty line must die by the end of the film (and the colour of her hair must be brunette). So bring back Lorelei and Viola: wise-cracking, lip-smacking femme fatales with the amusing ability to always land on somebody else's feet.

13

One

Every Man Needs a Mother

VIOLA LAKE!...Viola Lake...I wonder in how many of you that name rings a silvery bell? Viola Lake...cinema darling of the long ago; now only a shadow to those who watch television on the late, late, late show and find in those early films a counter-irritant to our present-day concern over the hydrogen bomb, atomic fallout, inflation, taxes, Freudian perplexities, and such.

Viola Lake! When first I loved her we were far apart—I in the top gallery of a cinema palace and she a luminous vision flitting across a screen. It is just possible that my daydreams of Viola were prompted by the fact that she was three thousand miles away in Hollywood and my homage did not need to interfere with my devotion to Mother who, in my boyish innocence, I deemed would always be first.

And then came a day, incredible though it still seems, when I loved Viola Lake in the flesh—when I held her in corporeal contact. Viola Lake and Elmer Bliss. Could such a possibility have ever been? No, it never could have—and yet it was.

Yesterday, by the time I finished putting my newspaper to bed for the week, the dawn had risen. I

*Viola Lake and Elmer Bliss. Could such
a possibility have ever been?*

stood looking out the window on to Main Street
inactivated as yet by our busy morning traffic. Presently
the hour of six struck and I turned the radio on for
news. The first items concerned the usual recount of
votes which inevitably follows a presidential election
…then the daily measure of invective from that arch-
dissembler, Khrushchev, after which was a routine list
of the previous day's motor crashes on our local
Freeway. But the morning's disasters closed with yet
another, small in universal interest perhaps, but
staggering to me. For the announcer said:

'Yesterday at the Motion Picture Country Club in
Van Nuys, Viola Lake, little remembered star of the
early films, slipped while taking her Saturday night bath
and broke her hip. The accident, although painful, was
not serious and the elderly actress is reported to be
resting cheerfully.'

I switched off the radio, deeply disturbed. For years,
my thoughts of her had been infrequent. But now a
rush of memories surged over me, bruising my heart
and bringing to life again the golden days of
Hollywood.

Viola Lake an inmate of the Motion Picture Country
Club! It was difficult to believe, for the term 'Country
Club' had been trumped up by the ever merciful Acting
Profession to glamorize a refuge for indigent film folk.
Oh, they live there in luxury, without a doubt, and are
comforted by alibis that they are 'resting between
pictures,' or 'organizing their own producing
companies,' or that their agents are 'arranging deals for
residual rights which will put them into a capital gains
bracket.' But just the same, the Viola Lake I had known

in her heyday had occupied her own million-dollar English mansion, the thatched roof of which had been specially constructed in the Cotswold Country and imported piecemeal, to the Film Capital.

As I stood there in my office musing about the past, it began to come over me that perhaps I had a mission in life, a mission to resurrect Viola's name and put her before the world as I knew her—not the Viola Lake of the scandal sheets but a work-a-day little lady trying desperately to live a simple life in which murder, divorce, and matrimonial lapses were never consciously planned.

But would I ever be equal to the task of explaining the bundle of contradictions which went to make up the enigma called Viola Lake? I must indeed confess to never having completely understood her myself. Am I equipped to tell the world at large the truth, the whole truth and nothing but the truth, about Viola? Well, let us see.

Before beginning her story, I must first recount the circumstances that brought me to Hollywood, where Fate ordained our paths would cross. These take me a long way from California to the Bronx area of New York, for it was there I first saw the light of day. My formal education had begun in public school No. 387, where I very early developed into being the one boy in the class who was always eager to recite; and when it came to the writing of compositions, never knew when to stop. At length, there arrived a momentous day when I discovered the public library, and while other children were wasting their time on the 'funnies,' I was far away with great thinkers like Ralph Waldo Trine, Mary Baker

Eddy, or Orsen Swett Marden (for I had a leaning toward philosophers of triple nomenclature, except in the case of my favourite, Wilhelmina Stitch of Great Britain, who made the truth more attractive by putting it into rhyme).

It was a small wonder that, on graduating from high school, I too felt ready to take up philosophy as a money-making proposition. And, full of youthful impetuosity, I shut myself up in my room to write an article.

I then started to try and interest the editors of New York City in my thinking. But the newspapers of that day were reeking with violence, and I soon learned there was no place for a writer whose optimism might have had a counteracting effect on the aftermath of World War I or the collapse of the stock market. After months of trying I would inevitably go home, crushed, to the Bronx. Then Mother would put her arms around me and say: 'Never mind, Elmer, all you need is to find the sort of people who will listen to you.'

Then I would remember the old truth that 'Mother is always right' and find strength to sit down and pen some more articles.

But after several years of striving, I was forced to realize that there was nothing for me in the New York area, for I refused to write the superficial wisecracks which pass for wit among the 'intelligentsia' there. However, I had sent a bundle of my work to a newspaper in Chicago and it had never been returned. Now it is a well-known fact among authors that when an editor retains material, he may be thinking it over. So, encouraged by this sign, I decided to go to Chicago for a personal interview with the editor. But on arriving at my destination, I discovered the newspaper office had been bombed.

This clarified the mystery as to why my manuscripts had not been returned. It moreover caused me to suspect that Chicago was no more interested than New York in the things of the spirit.

And in Chicago I had other experiences which disturbed me. Whenever I had thought about girls, if I thought about them at all, it was always as something apart. And in Chicago I woke up to the fact that there

I figured that in Southern California I might at least be warm.

were girls whom my attitude of reserve failed to discourage.

Chicago was really a nightmare. I finally had to send to Mother for money to come home. But when she sent the money, Mother suggested that instead of returning to the Bronx, I should proceed to Hollywood.

Mother had had her eye on Hollywood for some time. She was an ardent devotee of the movies, and after a long course of them, it dawned on her that Hollywood was just the spot for me. I hated to think of going so far from her and starting all over again in a strange place like Hollywood, but that year the winter had been more than usually rigorous and I figured that in Southern California I might at least be warm. So go I did, and Mother was to follow as soon as ever I could send for her.

I had scarcely arrived in Hollywood when, with body and soul warmed by the God-given sunshine, I sat down and penned a letter to *The Los Angeles Times*, describing the effect of sudden warmth on a tourist who had been cold all winter in the East. My letter was published! Encouraged, I wrote more letters and they were published. And then, fan mail began to arrive from strange people; for from the very beginning, I met with a response from the residents of Southern California who were eager to see an affirmation of their own ideas in print.

At length, one of my admirers, a Mr C. C. Cahoon, who owned a large printing company, asked if I would care to undertake, *for remuneration*, the writing of short bits of my philosophy to be used on a series of post cards to be illustrated with scenes of Southern

California—the beauty of each scene to be supplemented by some thought which would carry a message of sunshine to the addressee. To say that I fairly leaped at the opportunity would not be far from the truth.

But I soon found out that the task was not altogether easy. Uplifting thoughts came freely when the scene was one of Nature herself, as, for instance, some view of the purple hills of Hollywood or a riot of bougainvillia in tones of the fashionable new 'shocking pink.' But Mr Cahoon insisted on including views that made my work more difficult. One of his post cards was to be a picture of the Brown Derby Restaurant, which is architected in the form of a colossal derby hat. It was on this view that, after mature thought, I extemporized:

Where derby hats are so colossal, then, too, must be the daydreams conjured underneath them.

Mr Cahoon okayed my sentiment; and also a thought I conjured up for a picture of the Mary Pickford Tearoom, built in the giant effigy of Miss Pickford, with golden curls—and the entrance through the apron. Using this as my inspiration, I wrote:

The sunshine of Southern California has only one rival; the golden curls of America's Sweetheart.

C. C. liked the thought, as he also did one which I evolved to fit a view of the 'Cow' milk stations which are amusingly built in the form of cows with actually wagging tails. My response to this was:

Our cows not only provide milk, but also a conversation piece for its enjoyment.

Then, too, there was a picture of the 'Jail' Café, designed in replica of a county lockup, with the waiters in stripes; and where any instruments which might be used in jail-break, such as sharp knives, forks, or spoons, are not provided unless actually needed for the eating of the more solid nutriments. My comment on this was a mere quote:

In Hollywood, stone walls do not a prison make, nor iron bars a cage.[1]

But I will not enumerate the myriad types of Hollywood architecture Mr Cahoon insisted on including in the series—structures which, although amusing enough, scarcely provided a basis for idealistic thought.

However, I finished the series to the best of my ability, and the issue was flung upon the market. Did the citizenry of Hollywood desire optimism on their post cards? To use a vulgar expression, they did, and how! For the entire series sold out at once!!

This achievement of mine caused me to be approached by *Hollywood Tidings*, to write a column of my own comment on the day—again with remuneration!

Cynics love to say that the public cares only to read of sordid things. But I, for one, do not believe it. My column was successful from the start, though I told only of the good, the true, the beautiful.

I became, among other things, a champion of the Film Folk. And when their social gatherings ended in unpremeditated murder, I passed this over and devoted my space to telling of events like the first anniversary of a famous baby whose parents were known the world over and yet whose birthday cake consisted of a frosted bran muffin with one candle.

[1] Editor's Note: Mr Bliss' quotation predated the incarceration of Caryl Chessman.

At times when some film star was reported to have been found in a compromising situation with a person of the opposite sex, did I repeat the story? No! I devoted my space to telling how hostesses who invite 'Our Mary' to dine, receive a printed notice stating that she insists on sitting next to her *own* husband at the table.[1]

I repeated true stories of the lives of the unmarried film stars, which did much to change the public's notion of the 'wildness' of Hollywood. I told of the long musing of Lillian Gish, *alone* by the sea; of Aileen Pringle, curled up alone on a couch, deep in a volume of Joseph Hergesheimer; of Clara Bow, after a hard day's work at the studio, in bed by half-past nine with the 'Happiness Boys' coming through on the radio; and of Greta Garbo, 'siren' that she was, on a hike through a lonely gully—with her *milliner!*

I took up the cudgels for Hollywood as an Art Centre and reported the Sunday literary salons of the famous English authoress, Elinor Glyn. On one such occasion our hostess, lying on her tiger-skin rug, had told us how Viola Lake (*Viola Lake!*) had recently taken up reading…how she had stumbled on to a certain volume by the title of *Anna Karenina*[2] and how the novel (a tragedy) had impressed her so deeply she declared she would never again make a picture with the happy ending required by the box office. Now it so happened that she had just signed with a major studio to create the title role in the film version of *Pollyanna the Glad Girl*. But she now informed the producer that if Pollyanna didn't wind up getting run over by a train,

[1] This refers to the era preceding their divorce. *Ed.*
[2] A novel by a Russian author known as Alexander Tolstoy. *Ed.*

she would turn down the part. When the producer refused to make this change in the story-line, Miss Lake stamped her foot and walked out on her contract.

The screen, however, was not the only institution I befriended. I also went to the aid of religion, and when newspapers everywhere were ringing with accounts that our beautiful blonde evangelist, Aimee Semple McPherson, had spent a week in a secluded beach cottage with a certain young man, *I* told of the thousands upon thousands of old codgers who were able to spend *every night* with Aimee in her own glamorous Temple.

As time went on, new fields were opened to me. Radio took up my cheerful cry. My Sunday hour caused the name of Elmer Pastorfield Bliss to become the synonym for 'friend' in every household. I was at last a Force in a community which was actually over-crowded with Forces.

In only a few short months I was able to send for Mother. And together we made the first payment on a Spanish bungalow hidden away in one of the purple Hollywood hills.

However, *our* hacienda—Mother's and mine—was easy for any friend to find, for it overlooked the big electric '57' sign put up as an advertisement by a pickle company. There we were at last, Mother and I, honoured citizens of a Utopia of sunshine, spirit, art, and beauty—of Hollywood!

However, I do not wish to give the impression that my advocacy of life's better things was without annoying incidents, for opposing elements were present.

There was, in particular, a certain scoffing individual who had been a harmful influence in Hollywood for years. He was a newspaper feature-writer named Lansing Marshall, a correspondent of a San Francisco sheet which I will not dignify by name, and he had waxed and grown fat by seeking out and selling news of a vicious nature which defamed the fair name of Hollywood. Of course, San Francisco is jealous of our sunshine, our purple hills, our ideals, our growth, our industry, and most of all, of the prosperity resulting from them, and this certain scrivener delighted to attack them, each and every one.

I had always refrained from dignifying Lansing Marshall by any mention whatsoever in my column, and Marshall on his part concentrated on the infinite variety of his own pet subjects, such as murder, rape, hold-ups, drug addiction, kidnapping, bigamy, badger games, divorce, high-jacking, and bootleg activities. Thus, our fields of comment lay wide apart.

But on a certain morning in November there burst over our community like one of the thunderclaps which so frequently occur in less favoured climates, the sudden revelation of a more than usually disturbing murder case. In this instance the murderer, Calvin Barco (who, during his lengthy trial, came to be known by the pet name of Cal), admitted to slaying seven wives during a period of nine years, and to having buried the remains in sand dunes on the outskirts of Hollywood.

The sensation caused by the Barco case was unfortunate, for as far as anyone remembered, no one husband in our community had as yet murdered seven wives.

Well, in spite of my policy of dignified aloofness from such matters, I deemed that a short comment from my pen was almost called for. Here is my paragraph, as it appeared:

'How can such things as the Barco murders occur in this Heaven-blest spot, where mankind—daily kissed by Southern California sunshine—is endowed with all that is noblest in Nature and can boast of three times more hills than Rome; and where every prospect whispers of the nearness and goodness and clean-mindedness of God?'

That was the only mention I intended to make of the Barco murder. But I soon discovered that I should not have deviated at all from my position of dignified aloofness, for my paragraph brought forth an uncalled-for response from Lansing Marshall.

I fear I shall have to quote his vicious libel in order to lead up to an explanation of what later occurred. Here is what he said:

'On the matter of the Barco murders, Elmer Bliss, that gigantic intellect who evolved thoughts and theories which shake the very foundation of metaphysical speculation, now arises in all the majesty of his full-blown moral elephantiasis and, summoning into action every resource of his befuddled mentality, asks how any citizen of this "Heaven-blest" spot could possibly cut up seven wives with a set of rusty garden tools. Well, Mr Barco *did*, and if this fact gets in the way of Professor Bliss' clear, comprehensive and all-embracing view of the situation, perhaps I can shed a little light on the mystery of how our sun-kissed population is able to supply the most rare, varied, fantastic, interesting, and morbidly unique crimes that have ever tickled the craniums of a grateful reading public.'

Now this sardonic statement of Marshall's will illustrate what I mean when I say that his viewpoint is perverted, and gives an extremely distorted picture of life as it exists under the sunny skies of Southern California.

It is unfortunate Marshall must be quoted at all. But in order to clarify the various angles of the Barco case, and why I, with my deep aversion to murder, was drawn into it, it is necessary to explain his part in the proceedings.

However, forewarned is forearmed, and I do not fear that this man's crude misstatements will be taken seriously by anybody who ever stops to think.

Two

Can Sin be Perpetuated in the Sunshine?

DURING THE WEEK the Barco murders were disclosed, I was enlisting my energies in a project much more to my liking. It was a civic plan for changing the name of Hollywood Boulevard, during the forthcoming Yuletide season, to Santa Claus Lane, causing it to shine forth as a glittering symbol of Peace on Earth, Good Will Toward Men.

Naturally there were lively discussions for and against so radical a procedure. In the first place, it would necessitate the changing of street signs; the expense of replacing palm trees with pines; the cost of outfitting ever-so-many Santas; and the purchase of imitation snow and icicles, for these symbols of the eastern winter exist here only in the mild form of tinsel.

Now, my work as leader of the pro–Santa Claus Lane element had necessitated my rushing here, there and everywhere, and caused me for the moment to overlook the Barco murders. But Lansing Marshall was continuing his scurrilous articles to the detriment of our civic interest in Peace, the welfare of our fellow men, and good old Santa himself.

Other citizens of Hollywood, however, were keeping

A civic plan for changing the name of Hollywood Boulevard.

an eye on Marshall's activities, and one morning I received a telephone call asking me to meet a committee of public-spirited souls who had banded together to see if something could be done to hush him up.

Not wishing to neglect my Santa Claus Lane project which, at the moment, I deemed to be of greater import, I reacted to the summons with impatience. And yet that meeting changed the entire course of my life.

On reporting to the committee that eventful morning, I found it already in session and headed by my friend and admirer, C. C. Cahoon. It was then explained to me what had been done before I was called in. Here was the matter in a nutshell:

It seems the meeting had been hurriedly called when it was realized that Barco could never have murdered seven women without having a certain variety in his victims, and that this would inevitably drag into the forthcoming trial citizens from every walk of life in our community.

Now this would be cause enough for discomfort under the mildest of circumstances. But with Marshall writing up the case, seizing on every opportunity to delve into the affairs of our most sacred institutions, the whole thing was not to be thought of.

For instance, two members of our committee were members of the Hollywood Boulevard Association. To the HBA, Hollywood Boulevard was as sacred as the rue de la Paix to the ardent Frenchman or Bond Street to the staunch British patriot. And, unluckily, it had been the practice of Barco to make the acquaintance of his victims by accosting them on Hollywood Boulevard. This would give Marshall an opportunity to hint that Hollywood Boulevard was a street on which women could be 'picked up'—for other and worse purposes than murder, perhaps. *And that would never do!*

Also present at the meeting were representatives of a number of the unique religious sects in which Southern California so richly abounds. For it happened that the third of Barco's victims, Jessie Wisben, was of a devout nature and had joined a number of sects, one after the other; so the committee was understandably worried over what comments Marshall might make on them when they were dragged into the Barco case.

At one time Jessie Wisben had allied herself with the Holy Rollers who express their devotion by rolling on the floor of a cellar in downtown Los Angeles. Some sort of a romantic affair had developed from these contacts, and when Miss Wisben later found her affections to be unrequited, she renounced the creed. This was as far as the Holy Rollers figured in the Barco case, but it was far enough to give Marshall his chance to comment on the physical aspect of rolling and overlook its spiritual significance.

After leaving the Holy Rollers, Jessie Wisben had been drawn into an outdoor cult which worshipped in one of our more secluded gullies, the members of which, in a desire to get the largest possible surface contact with Mother Nature, wore a minimum of garments. Now it was feared that Marshall would make crude witticisms on this fact, concerning which we healthy-minded Hollywooders never had an obscene thought!

It was actually as a member of this cult that Jessie Wisben had first encountered Barco, in all the brevity of his Grecian peplum. However, Barco's intentions toward Jessie Wisben, aside from murder, were honourable, and he made the Wisben woman a proposal.

After marriage Cal and Jessie Barco lost their need of this cult, so to speak, and quit the colony. But even married life wears out its novelty in time and searching for new experiences, they one evening dropped into Angelus Temple, the spiritual home of the beautiful female divine, Aimee McPherson, and her Foursquare Gospel.

Here they witnessed a baptismal service which opened up to them a whole new world of thrills. Hip-

*As a member of an outdoor cult Jessie first encountered Barco.
His intentions, aside from murder, were honourable.*

deep in a concrete tank full of water and warmed to room temperature, stood the beautiful Aimee, her dripping robe clinging to every womanly curve as she pleaded with her disciples to renounce the flesh and give themselves over to a life of the spirit. Standing there in the spotlight, Aimee shouted through her microphone the thrilling news of the 'sheaves' as she gathered them in, supplying names and addresses so that the poor, the humble, and the obscure received a need of publicity they had dreamed of all their lives and had given up any hope of attaining.

Is it any wonder that Cal Barco and his bride didn't rest until they too could stand on that stage in the spotlight and hear Aimee shout into the microphone:

'Here is such a sweet honeymoon couple—Mr and Mrs Cal Barco, who live in Unit No. 7H of the Ginsberg Arms Motor Court. Oh, I wish you could see them now, all pure in their shining white robes! They are going to lead the life of the Spirit from now on, folks! They gave themselves body and soul to Angelus Temple on September the Sixth! *Mr and Mrs Cal Barco* is the name! Glory hallelujah!'

And then, with one forceful push of Aimee's capable hands, down they went into the tank, while the reverent throng cheered them to the echo. The Barcos, in fact, were a hit.

Now, after so dramatic an entrance into the Life of the Spirit, one might think that the regular nightly services at Angelus Temple would have proved an anticlimax to the Barcos. But that would only show one's ignorance of the Foursquare Gospel and of Aimee's infinite variety. For she was almost never the same, and so far as that went, neither was her gospel, nor the stage setting, which illustrated the reverent point she was trying to get over.

For instance, on one night the stage represented a storm at sea, with the altar disguised as a lighthouse, and Aimee, as the lovely lighthouse keeper in a sou'wester, with golden curls peeping from beneath an oilskin cap, beckoned the shipwrecked into her Heavenly Haven.

Or perhaps the next night the stage was set to represent a street intersection, and Aimee in police uniform, as a lovely traffic cop entered on a motor cycle, took her stand at the altar (cleverly transformed on this occasion into a stop-and-go signal) and directed the 'traffic' of the Spirit towards the Soul's Salvation.

At any rate, Barco and his bride were never bored with the Foursquare Gospel, and Barco himself remained a devout worshipper even after he murdered her.

However, it was unfortunate for the good name of Hollywood that during Barco's membership in Angelus Temple, Aimee McPherson had been involved in some sort of misappropriation of the church funds, had been indicted by the county grand jury for conspiracy to obstruct justice, and had unfortunately been named as co-respondent in a certain divorce action. And these contretemps were certainly what Marshall would feature in *his* account of the part played by religion in the Barco murders.

His irreverent mind would also gloss over the fact so significant of our spiritual capacity, that before reaching Southern California, Mrs McPherson had wandered across the United States for years, looking for a place on which permanently to light. But in each and every city of the land, she had run out of converts in about two weeks. Only on reaching Los Angeles did she find a supply which never gave out. And this, on the very border of 'wicked Hollywood!'

But to get back to our committee meeting…The last member of the group to arrive that morning was Benjamin Goldmark, head of Goldmark Motion Picture Productions; and to make this day the most portentous of my life thus far, Goldmark was accompanied by—Viola Lake.

Oh, I could easily have met Miss Lake before, for she was anything but exclusive, but I had purposely avoided her because quite frankly, I was afraid. What had I that might be of interest to a girl like her? I had always thought of myself as lacking in the type of small talk which might interest a carefree child of the cinema. But I was now to learn that I was utterly wrong in my supposition. For Viola seemed to draw me out, so that I presently found myself commenting on the lighter type of subjects—subjects which had no bearing on the meeting whatsoever. In fact, Goldmark finally had to interrupt and remind us that 'it was no time for twattle,' a chastisement we rather richly deserved, I fear. For I was now to learn that Miss Lake herself stood in danger of being involved in the Barco case.

It seems that one of the women married and murdered by Barco was a certain Mrs Geiger who for several years had been Miss Lake's confidential cook. Well, Mrs Geiger evidently had had very little work to do, as Miss Lake was frequently away from home for breakfast, luncheon, and dinner. With time hanging heavily upon her hands, Mrs Geiger had kept a diary and having no social life of her own—that is, until she met Barco—she had jotted down the doings of Miss Lake.

This diary had been found and was now in the possession of the district attorney. Suppose he allowed it to be read in court! What then? Why, Marshall would, of course, reprint it—with any amount of his own particular brand of *double entendre*!

I don't really know why, but I must confess that in spite of my generally sunny spirit the case began to take on a rather sombre aspect. However, C. C. was not cognisant of my doubts, and now he asked me to take the chair and inject a little of my well-known optimism into the meeting. So take the chair I did.

'My friends,' I said, addressing them, 'I have a thought! Why does Hollywood not overlook the Barco murders and put its energies into our Santa Claus Lane project in a bigger, better, brighter way than we had even planned? Let us place a giant effigy of Santa on the roof of every building on Hollywood Boulevard; let us unloose asbestos snow from an aeroplane the full length of the street; let every glamorous screen star spend one day riding up and down with Santa in an open sleigh, as "Santa's Sweetheart." In other words, let us smother the Barco publicity with a Hollywood Christmas such as this old world has never seen!'

My suggestion was greeted by applause from every member of the committee save Goldmark, who spoke up and said: 'Wait a minute, young fellow; have you read what this guy Marshall wrote last week?'

I told Goldmark that I had not, as indeed there were better things for me to think of. He then handed me a newspaper clipping with the advice that I had better look it over. Well, I read through Marshall's first paragraph, and I must say it seemed to be of not too uncomplimentary a nature; for it said:

'In order to understand the amazing breed which has been achieved in Southern California, it is necessary to go into its pioneer history and show how, from the very start, it has been composed of elements which were bound to make it unique in the history of the human race.'

On finishing the paragraph, I took the opportunity to digress and say that I saw little at which to take exception. We were indeed unique.

But Goldmark told me to read further. So on I read:

'The early settler in Southern California was altogether different from the pioneer who went to the northern part of the state in the covered wagon of '49. This fellow was capable of being touched by the spirit of adventure, and he also needed a fair quota of guts before facing a pretty tough trip. Then too there were difficulties on the way which served as a final sifting-out process, for the only ones to reach the goldfields had to possess enough brains and stamina to outwit Indians, buffalo stampedes, coyotes, hunger, thirst, disease, and other impediments.'

Now even this second paragraph seemed to be fair enough. But Goldmark said to read on and 'get the stinger' in Marshall's next paragraph. Well, here it is:

'But—the great swarm of settlers who squatted in Southern California came *after* the railroad was built.

There was no lure of gold to stir this pioneer's imagination, for the unbounded natural resources of this section were not yet realized. So he was led, not by the spirit of adventure, but by the fact that he was a failure in his home community. And in order to get to his new field where he would find cheap living and a warm climate, all he needed was sufficient brains to procure a third-class ticket on a train, and a paper box full of enough acrid lunch to last six days in a fetid tourist Pullman car. As a matter of fact, he was probably supplied with both ticket and lunch, free, by relatives who were keenly interested in his departure for distant parts.'

I had to admit that this began to look prejudiced and I started to say so, in no qualified terms, when Goldmark signalled me to continue, which I did.

'Now one might think, offhand, that such a supply of low-grade mental stamina would have produced a humdrum civic spirit. For naturally this citizen, left in his native state, would have been held in check by an everyday struggle to make a bare living. But in the rich lap of Southern California and competing with morons no cleverer than himself, all he had to do was to reach out and take, for sustenance was free for the taking.

'And so, unburdened of financial worries, he blossoms forth, manufactures gaudy clothing, freak architecture, cosmetically aided blondes, rowdy exhibitionist religions, and all the other bawdy amusements which his aesthetically five-year-old brain can conjure up.

'And as in the case of Cal Barco, under the amazing, life-giving, rejuvenating sun of Southern California, his feeble moral nature wakes, leaps up, kicks off its nightshirt and dances out into murder, rape, kidnapping, incest, and other crimes of the most intriguing incident, making life full of robust interest for the lowly student of human nature like myself.'

Dazed, I finished Marshall's scurrilous libel, the hot blood of indignation mounting to my cheeks. Then, hands clinched, I faced them all and said:

'This is outrageous!'

And it was outrageous! But the rub was—what could be done? The article had been published in San Francisco, our enemy city of the north. Marshall's words were already scattered far and wide by the noxious winds of San Francisco, which are so different from the gentle zephyrs of the southern area of our state.

As I stood there, stymied, Viola spoke up and I was now to learn for the first time of her serious side. For the little star had a suggestion which was that I should personally talk to Marshall and try to make him drop his negative approach to the Barco murders. Addressing the entire roomful she went on to say how much she admired my column—that she had one of my mottoes framed, hanging over her bed, and had grown to be superstitious about it, for she noticed that when she did wrong it sometimes fell down.

Galvanized by her thrilling compliment, I thanked Viola. Then squaring my shoulders I faced the committee.

'Friends,' I said, 'if you will appoint me your spokesman, I *shall* go to Marshall and appeal to his better nature.'

I then reminded them of a precept of Will Rogers, our own philosopher of the movie world, who once wrote for publication: 'I never *knew* a man I couldn't love.'[1]

I continued: 'By the time I shall have finished with Marshall, it is my earnest belief that he will cease his adverse comment on the Barco case.'

Applause broke out and continued until Goldmark, always full of hardheaded doubt toward any idea which happened not to be his own, spoke up and said that the Goldmark Film Corporation was willing to try and jog Marshall's 'better nature.'

And so the meeting broke up in a far, far different mood from that in which it had opened, for as C. C. Cahoon so forcefully remarked: 'We can relax, now that Elmer is on the job!'

Well, augmented by one more reason for devotion to the Southland in the dainty person of Viola Lake, I walked out into the sunshine and headed for Marshall's stamping ground, the Brown Derby Restaurant, there to face him in a plea for Hollywood and for *her!*

[1] This was before the advent of Hitler and Eichmann. As a matter of fact, it is unlikely that Mr Rogers would ever have acknowledged an introduction to either of them. *Ed.*

Three

I Take Up the Cudgels for Purity

As I stepped out on to the Boulevard, I thought it wise not to encounter Marshall without first letting my thoughts take form. So I decided to walk to the 'Derby' and proceeded to park my sports car under one of the red plush, gold-fringed canopies of a garage. Then I proceeded down Hollywood Boulevard on foot. Hollywood Boulevard! What a highway! There it stretched like a strip of artistic carpetry which had been flung down in carnival spirit, as if in preparation for a feast. And it was indeed a feast of beauty, for that old street teemed with girls from every country on earth, whose friends had said to them in every living tongue: 'With your looks, you ought to be in pictures.'

Hollywood Boulevard! What Romance stalked its seething sidewalks! Today one of its myriad little blondes was a mere 'car hop.' Tomorrow she might be a cinema star of world renown—discovered overnight by some motion-picture director.

I passed Grauman's two-million-dollar Chinese Theatre, in front of which were the footprints of famous film folk, preserved for all time to come by having the stars step into the cement before it hardened. (And, in the case of Douglas Fairbanks, the rascal stood on hands as well.)

And the shops of Hollywood Boulevard! How they glowed with every lovely thing our artistry could devise for the adornment of our maidenhood, from dainty, diamond-studded pocket-handkerchiefs to exquisite ermine bathing ensembles! For Hollywood styles were free from the traditions which hamper the rue de la Paix. Our fashion designers let their love of Beauty run riot among ruffles, spangles, puffs, feathers, fancy furs, and trimmings of every hue and tint, to adorn the healthy sun-nourished bodies of our girls.

Walking briskly along, drinking it all in, I couldn't resist the temptation to stop, as some bit of Art or other caught my eye in the shop windows. Here, a life-size marble statue of classic female form divine, holding up a bowl of goldfish, there a hand-painted picture of an

Today, a car-hop. Tomorrow, a cinema star.

Indian maiden under the harvest moon, done in phosphorescent paint which would reveal its beauty even more sumptuously after one turned the lights out.

And in each and every window interesting testimonials from great motion-picture stars, written on their own intriguing photographs. Among them I twice caught glimpses of Viola Lake, and I fear I loitered rather longer than I should have in the presence of that smiling visage. On one of the photographs Miss Lake had written a witticism to her hairdresser. It said: 'To darling Nino who has "made" more blondes than any guy in Hollywood.' The other photograph was an Art study, posed in filmy drapes which revealed her lovely form, and the message read: 'With fondest love to Mr Dodd for the way he fixed my plumbing.'

Well, I presently realized that the old street had once more worked its witchery on me, for I had gathered calmness, strength, and confidence with which to face our enemy. Forcing my footsteps into quicker pace, I entered the old 'Derby' and looked about. Again a thrill! For at the luncheon hour it seethed with the collected beauty, brains, and wit of the entire motion-picture industry. There, in person, eating lunch like other people, sat famous film stars, scenarists, directors, composers, lyric writers, artists, designers, and executives. Added to these there were always a few visiting geniuses and even members of royalty from the outer world. 'And' (to quote from the book by Perley Poore Sheehan, *Hollywood as a World Centre*), 'among them will be one, or two, or three, more widely known than any human beings have ever been known since the world began.'

Do I have to repeat such magic names as Doug, Mary, Cecil, Charlie, Jackie, and Gloria and compare them to the less universally famous, such as Voltaire, Goethe, Florence Nightingale, Garibaldi, Spinoza, Kosciusko, Parnell, and Madame Curie? And do I also have to point out that the latter group lived in *different* countries at *different* periods of time, while the former were all alive at once, in the one single metropolis of Hollywood?

Well, be that as it may, the fact remained that there was *one* enemy to culture in the midst of those world-famous souls eating lunch in the 'Derby,' and I had come to plead with him. So I asked the headwaiter to lead me to Mr Marshall.

Now I had never met him personally, so on arriving at the table where he sat—most fortunately, alone—I at once confronted him, saying: 'Marshall, I am Bliss!'

Marshall acknowledged my introduction with a rather friendly hospitality, for which I must say I was unprepared. Then, to my surprise, he asked me if I would do him the honour of joining him for luncheon. His invitation was so insistent that finally I sat down and although of little appetite ordered prune whip and a cup of tea. Then, I forthwith got down to business.

'Marshall,' I began, 'you *say* that you despise Hollywood and all we stand for.'

He replied that this just about sized the matter up.

'And yet, Marshall,' I went on, 'you have only to look about you at this moment, to realize that there are more brains *right here* under this old Brown Derby, if I may be allowed a facetious simile, than have ever been collected in one spot, at one time, in the entire history of the world!'

I confronted Lansing Marshall, an enemy to culture amidst world-famous souls eating lunch in the Brown Derby.

'Wait a minute, Bliss, old boy,' he broke in. 'I'm afraid you're heading just the least trifling bit toward hyperbole.'

Well, I didn't wish the man to think I was prejudiced, so I spoke up and conceded that other periods in the world's history had enjoyed their famous groups. For instance, Queen Elizabeth had been surrounded by Shakespeare, Mary Queen of Scots, Sir Walter Raleigh, and Sir Francis Drake. But I told him that the Elizabethan Era would certainly have been improved had it enjoyed the spirit of optimism which glows over our intelligentsia here in Hollywood.

'Given *that*,' said I to Marshall, 'the Elizabethan Period might have been productive of more *cheerful* results. Of course, Elizabeth herself was a lifelong virgin, and to that splendid fact Hollywood is willing to pay full homage. But had the Elizabethan Era been granted a touch of Hollywood idealism, the tragedies of Shakespeare might have carried a more pleasing message; Lear and Shylock might have found solace in a calm old age; Mary Queen of Scots might have got off on Probation; Raleigh might have thought twice before he popularized tobacco (a solace to those who use it in moderation, but a cause of untold harm to others); and Drake, the great admiral, might have compromised with the *Armada*—a peace without victory—and spared the lives of hundreds of Spanish sailor boys!'

Well, as I finished my unanswerable argument, I could see that Marshall was a trifle dazed, and felt that I 'had him on the hip.' So, quickly following up my advantage, I launched into naming famous artists and literati who glorified our Hollywood spirit. Folks like Ralph Waldo Trine, Carrie Jacobs Bond, Rita Green Breese, Esther Birdsall Darling, Marah Ellis Ryan, and Ferdinand Pinney Earle, who never put pen to paper, scalpel to clay, paint to canvas, or toe to dance stage, without launching into a message of hope.

I then quoted to Marshall another passage from *Hollywood as a World Centre* which states: 'These people have made of Hollywood such a city of refuge for writers of all kinds, dreamers of all kinds—not artists and philosophers only, but straight friends of humanity—as never the world has seen. It suggests not so much the Venice of the Doges, nor the Athens of Pericles, nor Byzantium the New Rome, as it does a beatified combination of all of these.'

I stopped for a moment to note the effect of this quotation on Marshall. He looked not only dazed, but positively limp. So, feeling that I had found a clue to something inherently good in him, I went on.

'Marshall,' I said, 'you *pretend* to despise Hollywood! Yet how can you live in a place where you can't enjoy life?'

'Who said I didn't enjoy it here?' he asked. I answered with yet another question: 'How can a man enjoy what he despises?' And, like Socrates, I felt I had confounded him.

However, I reckoned without taking his inherent cynicism into account.

'Just a moment, pal,' he answered. 'Don't ever make a mistake about my *enjoying myself* in Hollywood! There isn't another spot on earth where I could obtain one-tenth the mental, moral, spiritual, and aesthetic joy that I get right here!'

'To begin with,' he went on, 'when I wake in the morning and open my newspaper, I find that such a devastating event as the St Valentine Day massacres in Chicago has been crowded off the front page by news that Southern California spent the foregoing day wallowing in sunshine, although it has been snowing in the East. This arrangement of the news helps to cheer a man up no end.

'Then,' continued Marshall, 'I turn perhaps to the section of the newspaper devoted to the arts, and find that some bit of distressing news, such as, let us say, the death of Eleanora Duse, has been crowded into two lines at the bottom of the page by the breath-taking announcement that Tony, the Horse, has just signed his new movie contract, with a large picture of Tony, pen tied to hoof, doing it. And I begin to feel that Art has overcome the handicap of Duse's death, and that all is well in the world of the Aesthetics.

'Scores of similarly soothing items cast about me an aura of sweet satisfaction and I realize that the blithe spirit of Hollywood cannot be dimmed by the sordid realities of the outside world. By the time I have finished my newspaper, I am so cheered up and happy that I wouldn't exchange my humble bedroom in the Ambassador Hotel for a love nest on Park Avenue.

'And that brings me to yet another advantage of life in Hollywood,' he continued. 'In an ordinary American city there is a limited supply of negotiable girlhood. But Hollywood is different. The movies have drawn thousands of beauteous girls here from every quarter of the globe. A very small percentage fills up the requirements of the cinema, and what are left over flow into business channels so that a man cannot go into a drugstore, restaurant, cigar stand, or even an oil station without having his eye tickled by ravishing womanhood. And you suggest that I don't enjoy myself in Hollywood! Why, my dear man, your ignorance of simple, uncomplicated psychology in a case like mine is actually irritating!'

As Marshall came to the close of his cynical tirade, it began to dawn on me that my method of attack had not exactly led to the point I had wished to attain. At any rate, it seemed rather advisable to change tactics.

'Marshall,' I said, 'I'm going to get down to Hecuba. There are certain things likely to crop up when the Barco murder case comes to trial which we—well, we wish to have soft pedalled in the newspapers. Among those who are worried are the executives of the

Goldmark Film Corporation. They are prepared to do anything within reason to avoid unfavourable publicity, and hope you will abandon your comment on the case!'

The man actually seemed indignant.

'Look here, Bliss,' he exclaimed, 'do you realize that this offer has all the earmarks of a bribe? I resent it as an affront to my moral status!'

His assumption of a 'moral status' caused my ire to flare up.

Looking him squarely in the eye, I asked: 'Marshall, have you no scruples about *earning a living* in a community which you daily deride?'

'Scruples?' he exclaimed. 'Nonsense! I don't have to *earn* a living *here*. It forces itself on me! You don't think a mug like myself has to *work* in this town. Why, with a mental equipment which allows me to tell the difference between hot and cold, I stand out in this community like a modern day Cicero.

'Dropped into any other city of the world, I'd rate as a possibly adequate night watchman. And let's be fair, old pal, you yourself, a leader of public thought in Hollywood, wouldn't have sufficient mental acumen anywhere else to hold down a place in a breadline!

'So you can go back to that noble lineup of modern Venetians, twentieth-century Athenians, and neo-classical Romans and report that Lansing Marshall is in the Barco case to stay!'

Well, so be it! In that eventuality the die was cast. However, there was one thing I might yet do *for her* and, speaking in tones of earnest appeal, I asked: 'Marshall, will you promise to bar all mention of Viola Lake from your account of the case?'

Now he seemed actually to bridle. 'As a newspaper man, you know what it means to let your paper down. Naturally, I'll be as gallant as I can to the little lady. I've always been very fond of her. But it's a case where "I could not love Vi Lake so much, loved I not honour more."'

I went cold all over. For the fact dawned on me that it was useless to argue any further and that I might just as well go home.

So we parted at the door of the 'Derby,' enemies still. He went his way, once again to dip his pen into poisoned ink while I went mine, to conjure up some other scheme to thwart him.

Well, as I walked back along Hollywood Boulevard, it presently began to seem that the next best move on my part would be to talk to Viola Lake herself and find out just what might be contained in the Geiger diary. Then came the idea—why not ask Miss Lake to our home for dinner, after which I could get her to tell me, in a heart-to-heart, everything she had ever done that might be misconstrued and used against her.

I confess to a quickening of pulse as I stepped into a drugstore and telephoned Viola at the studio. The response to my invitation was a heart-warming 'yes indeedy.' And she ended by graciously saying: 'Thank you, *Elmer*, for your lovely hospitality.'

Then I found myself back on Hollywood Boulevard, excited as I had never been when I used to watch Viola in the lush atmosphere of a Bronx movie palace or—in my Chicago phase—sat gazing at her in a humble nickelodeon of the Loop district.

Four

A Homebody Without a Home

FOR YEARS MOTHER had fretted about my lack of interest in girls and now that I had asked one in for the evening, she was almost as excited as I myself. She spent the whole day in preparation. Bless my soul, if she didn't even go out and buy a hammock to string up on the porch!

When I went to call for Viola that evening at the Cotswold mansion she had built herself in the bosom of Beverly Hills, she was waiting on the porch, dressed (as I believe the fashion reporters would say) in a gay, red tulle frock, with satin slippers and tennis socks to match, a silver headdress on the Russian order, and an ermine evening wrap with white fox collar, garnished with the inevitable shower of orchids. I bundled her into my sports roadster and we were off.

As I drove Viola through the winding roadways of the Beverly district in the dusk, the soft spring air heavily laden with the perfume of orange blossoms, I had to admit there was a very different 'something' in my sensations than I had ever noted while driving Mother.

We reached home—not so elegant as the one we had just left—but Mother was waiting at the doorway, her spangled evening gown aglitter in the reflection of the giant '57' sign that rotated on our hillside.

Viola was charming. Her constant refinement delighted me. We sat for cocktails of California tomato juice, and were soon deep in conversation which ranged in subject matter from antique furniture to flowers, bird life (both wild and tame), and, as always, the climate of Southern California.

During dinner I could not help but admire the little film star's *savoir-faire*, for nothing could have been more elevating than the table talk. I was actually surprised to hear this child of the lighter form of film fare make such remarks as: 'I think that Bolshevism is bad for the people,' or 'I think that the motion-picture palaces are the cathedrals of the future.'

My worries about Viola's reputation began to melt away. Surely here was a character that could stand the searchlight of investigation. I began to 'let myself go' a little further in my inclination to admire her.

Once dinner was over, Mother fairly rushed us on to the porch. She gestured Viola into the new hammock, placed me beside her, tucked us both in with cushions, and said:

'Now, I'm going to run over to Mrs Beebe's for an evening of bridge, so you two dear children just enjoy yourselves!' And giving Viola a parting pat, she left us together *en tête-à-tête*.

There we sat, high on our hillside, in alternative darkness and light, as the '57' flashed on and off. For some little while we remained in silence, gazing down on the myriad far-off lights that make Hollywood such a shimmering shower by night. And then Viola, in a gesture which smacked of the impulsive, finally reached over and took my hand. I confess to a shade of uneasiness, for there were unpleasant matters to be gone into first. So dropping the little hand, I rose and braced myself for the business of the evening.

Viola reached over and took my hand. I confess to a shade of uneasiness at her gesture.

First broaching the matter of the upcoming Barco trial, I earnestly assured Viola that I meant to do everything in my power to protect her reputation.

'But before I enter the lists in your behalf, dear child,' I said, 'I've got to be prepared. I've got to know what's in that Geiger woman's diary. So I want you to put your memory to work and tell me every occurrence of a personal and private nature that took place in your activities from the first moment you met her.'

I glanced at Viola to note her reaction to what I had asked. She was biting her lip, and it was rather clear that I had evoked unpleasant thoughts. So I went back to the hammock, and this time *I* took *her* hand, but it was only in a well-defined spirit of protection.

'Come on now, girl!' I pleaded, using my male authority. 'Tell me the whole story!'

Viola began to look uncomfortable in the extreme. A lassitude had also set in on her; her eyes were dull and dimmed; she swallowed once or twice and finally said:

'Well, Elmer, it's quite a long story, so I think I'd like to have a glass of water.'

'Only water?' I asked, thinking that perhaps the poor child might need a stimulant, under the trying circumstances; a cup of coffee perhaps.

'That's all,' she said and tossed a wan little smile in my direction. So off I went to fetch the pure refreshment of her choice. When I returned I noted that Viola had 'freshened up' miraculously. She must have been 'titivating' in my absence, for colour had returned to her cheeks and her dancing eyes now fairly sparkled with vitality. She made a place for me beside her, arranged the cushions so that I would be 'comfy,' and then launched into her experiences with Mrs Geiger. And I believe that a more insufferable set of circumstances has never been unfolded.

'Elmer,' she said, 'all my troubles started when I began to build my big English estate in Beverly Hills. Before that, I was very happy in a motor court. But the publicity department was always having to photograph me on somebody else's gorgeous estate because I didn't have one of my own. So I decided to build an English mansion on account of my ancestors having come from Manitoba.

'Well, there was a famous London architect named Sir Arnold Endicott, paying Hollywood a visit, so I went to see him and said: "Sir Endicott, I want you to build me a typical five-hundred-thousand-dollar English mansion with a thatched roof."

'Well, at first he said he couldn't do it, because the English never allowed anything to be thatched except a cottage. So I asked him what he thought my personality suggested. Well, after he considered the subject for a while, he finally said: "By Jove, little woman, you're right after all. A five-hundred-thousand-dollar mansion with a thatched roof is just the ticket!" So I thanked him for the compliment and he went to work designing it.

'Well, after it got built, the studio gave me six weeks to go to London and buy English antiques for it. And they sent a camera crew and a publicity lady to photograph and interview me while I went shopping. But when I finished, the crew left and the publicity lady collapsed and went into a nursing home. So there I was, all alone in London, waiting for a boat to get me back to Hollywood for my next picture.

'And, Elmer, with nothing to do, I always seem to get in trouble. So one morning, I sat down to look at my list and see if I had forgotten anything. Then I got the idea of importing a housekeeper, of the dignified English type we get from Central Casting, and went to the clerk at the hotel to ask if he knew where I could find one. Well, he did, and he said he thought she would give satisfaction as she had worked for Americans before and was able to stand kind treatment.

'That afternoon the housekeeper showed up at my suite and it was Mrs Geiger. I started by asking her what American she had worked for last and she said: "Let's not go into that, miss. She was a 'orrid lady." Then I asked her about some of the others, and Mrs Geiger said they were all "'orrid." Well, I began to think that maybe Mrs Geiger was anti-American. But I decided to put her to the test by inquiring about someone English who I *knew* was all right. So I said: "What is your opinion of Queen Victoria, Mrs Geiger?" And Mrs Geiger answered: "Oh, miss, I didn't 'old with 'er at all! She was too full of honest hintentions. I don't call it 'uman."

'Well, naturally I was shocked and decided not to engage her. But then I got to thinking that Hollywood is so full of "yes people" it might be beneficial to have somebody in my environment who was able to say "no". And the upshot was that I had to go and import a pessimist to Hollywood.

'And looking back on it now, I realize that everything that happened was an omen *not to take Mrs Geiger to Hollywood*. First of all, we had to take the boat at a place called Plymouth. So we went down there the day before. And no sooner did we get into the hotel than Mrs Geiger started to complain about the "spigots" in the bathroom. She said they were "'ateful."

'So I suggested that we go out and take a walk, and started to put on my hat. And then Mrs Geiger said, "Oh, don't wear that 'at, miss. You look awful!" Well, I felt my character was being developed, so I unpacked a hat she didn't mind so much, and we started on our walk.

'Well, the only thing in the way of entertainment at

Plymouth was to drop tuppences in some penny-in-the-slot machines on the dock. But when I suggested we take advantage of them, Mrs Geiger said: "I don't 'old with penny-in-the-slot machines, miss. All they want is your tuppence, and what comes out is twaddle."

'Well, her pessimism took all the fun out of Plymouth, so I decided we might just as well go to bed.

'The next morning about eleven, I opened my eyes and saw Mrs Geiger come into my room with a smile on her face for the first time since I met her. So I asked what had finally made her happy and she said: "Oh, miss, I've been watching the people come in off the pleasure boats, and *they're all sick!*"

'Well, *that* remark was really a hint that Mrs Geiger was what they call a "sadist," but just the same, I took her clear to Hollywood!

'After we got settled in my new house I tried to make things pleasant for Mrs Geiger, because I thought she might be homesick. Sometimes I used to say, "Who do you think you're going to see at dinner tonight? Gloria Swanson!" And she'd answer back, "I seen 'er already, miss, on the Boulevard—all dressed up like a tuppenny 'am bone."

'Why, Elmer, you wouldn't believe the things that woman could hate! She hated harmless little orphans and Easter bunnies, and the Hollywood Passion Play, and Rin-Tin-Tin, and Grauman's Chinese, and even Baby Peggy. So I finally got fed up and I told her she could go. *And, at that, she said to me*: "Oh, no, miss. I think I'll stay!"

'I didn't like her tone when she said it, and I soon discovered why, because it came out that Mrs Geiger had been keeping a diary of everything I did from the moment she came to work for me. And she hinted that if I discharged her she would turn her diary over to the Church Alliance and the Federated Women's Clubs.

'Well, Elmer, what I went through the next two years was almost unbelievable. Mrs Geiger not only stopped working, but she used to give the other servants several days off a week, so they could keep her company. Sometimes they'd all take my car and go off on weekends to the Mexican bullfights in Tia Juana.

'There was never a bite to eat in the house. After spending five-hundred-thousand-dollars on an *English* mansion, I couldn't even get a cup of tea!

'Sometimes after a hard day's work, I'd come back from the studio and ring for Mrs Geiger and say: "Mrs Geiger, I'm hungry!" And she'd say: "Why don't you bake yourself a cake?"

'And Elmer, she pronounced the word "cake" like a word I refuse to let anybody use in my home, out of reverence for the religion of Mr Goldmark.

'And sometimes, Elmer,' Viola continued, 'I'd think of the millions of film fans who believe the lives of we motion-picture stars are a bed of rosebuds, without ever knowing the heartaches we go through!

'But finally Mrs Geiger took to spending a great deal of time away from home. And one day she went away and never came back. I looked high and low for her diary, but she had taken all of her things with her and a good many of mine

'Well, I got a whole set of new servants, and food began to be served in the house once more. But just when I was beginning to feel relaxed and cosy in my own home, they caught Mr Barco, and it came out that the last woman he married and murdered was *Mrs Geiger*! I could hardly believe my ears when I read it. I could understand Mr Barco's wanting to kill Mrs Geiger, but why he ever wanted to *marry* her, I can never figure out.

'Well, of course, I began to wonder more and more what had become of her diary. Then finally one day I learned that it had been found and had fallen into the hands of the district attorney to be used as evidence at the murder trial. So I got rather worried and told Mr Goldmark about it.

'So now Elmer, you know everything and there isn't any more to tell.'

The story stunned me, but even so, it was still far from 'everything' I was required to know. Perturbed, I rose from the hammock and started to pace the porch.

'Viola, what accusations could Mrs Geiger possibly have made against you in that diary with any shadow of foundation?'

After a momentary reluctance Viola spoke. 'Well, Elmer,' she said, 'the thing that worries me most is that Mrs Geiger struck up a friendship with a gentleman I know named Mr Cream.'

An ominous chill stole over me at the mention of that name. 'Do you mean the character called Neal Cream?'

She nodded. I was aghast. For I had seen this individual hovering around various fringes of the industry. 'You had a…a romance with *Neal Cream?*' I gasped.

'Oh, no, Elmer,' she cried, 'it isn't *that*…it's something else.' And then Viola went into a confused explanation, the purport of which was that Cream was in the habit of supplying her with headache pills which were unprocurable at the pharmacy without a prescription.

An icy hand clutched at my heart.

'Great good heavens, child!' I exclaimed. 'Do you realize the evil-minded Geiger woman might have described those pills in her diary as *dope*?'

'Well, that's what I'm afraid of,' Viola faltered.

'How much of this does your employer, Goldmark know?' I asked her.

'Well,' she replied, 'up to now he's only been scared of my romances. He hasn't heard about the pills yet.'

It was awful to think of what the result of this disclosure would be on Goldmark. For those were the days when fear used to clutch at the heart of Hollywood every time one of our stars ever made a lapse from the norm.

Today in the sixties our temerity is hard to realize. For now the allure of moral turpitude has been established; now that a certain Southern playwright has confirmed the entertainment value of incest, castration, and cannibalism, our idols feel free to publicize such peccadillos as drug addiction or even rape, which, as in the case of a most important blonde star, took place at the age of ten.

As I sat there dazed over Viola's peril, an overpowering impulse surged up in me. It was to get her out of the house before something terrible happened on our own premises. For I confess to a disturbing sensation that she belonged in that category of unfortunates who serve as a magnet for disaster to anyone in their vicinity. I went to the door and held it open.

'Go get your wrap on, child,' I said. 'I'll fetch Mother from the Beebes' and *we'll both* see you home!'

Just the same my heart ached for Viola as, with tears welling into her eyes, she humbly got up from the hammock and entered the house. Then, like a shot I dashed across the road and made for the Beebes'.

They were deep in their bridge game when I rushed into the parlour and, with blanched face, stated: 'Mother, I need you!'

Mother rose from the card table and I sensed a certain note of impatience as she replied: 'Oh all right, Elmer!'

We spoke a brief 'good night' to the mystified Beebes. As I dragged Mother back to the house, I merely announced that it was prudent to have chaperonage when I went to deposit Viola at her home. For, at this point, I felt that the only ones to be told Viola's secret were Mr Goldmark and the Hollywood Board of Commerce.

I bundled Viola into the front of my sportster, boosted Mother into the rumble-seat, and off we went. Viola said nothing on the way home, but I could sense an inclination to 'snuggle up' for sympathy. Steeling myself against encouraging her, I remained rigid.

When I saw Viola Lake through her carved oaken door, I breathed a sigh of relief. But the relief was momentary. As I started back to my car, the dark shadow cast by that disturbing diary began to hover over me. Poor Viola! What was going to happen to her

*I rushed into the Beebes' parlour and cried out,
'Mother, I need you!'*

next? And Hollywood—my Hollywood! Would it ever
recover from the scandal and calumny that threatened
to besmirch it?

Five

The Brighter Side of Murder

THE FOLLOWING MORNING a distressing ordeal lay ahead of me. Not even the California sunshine could gild the fact that I must go to Viola's employer and break the news to him that the star he had spent millions to publicize as America's Favourite Film Flapper might be revealed in the forthcoming Barco trial as having slipped into the use of some habit-forming drug.

All the night before I had lain awake thinking, thinking. And finally at long last I had evolved a plan. But I would have to convince Goldmark that my plan was *right*. For there was a touch of defeatism in the man's nature which might be difficult to overcome.

When dawn came I telephoned C. C. Cahoon at his home and told him a crisis had arisen in the Barco affair, and that before acting on it, I needed moral support.

'Will you round up some of the boys from the Hollywood Boulevard Association and meet me in Goldmark's office at ten?' I asked. C. C., as usual, said I might count on him.

Too impatient to wait until ten o'clock, I entered Goldmark's outer sanctum quite early, and found it already full of suppliants. I was motioned to a seat by a glamorous secretary, and then realized I was expected to await my turn.

This would never do! I proceeded to tell the secretary that I must see Mr Goldmark *at once* on a crisis which meant life and death to the motion-picture industry.

With an attitude which seemed to suggest that matters-of-life-and-death-to-the-motion-picture-industry were rather more the rule around there than the exception, she entered the inner sanctum.

Presently she emerged. 'Mr Goldmark says to tell you that there are seventeen crisises ahead of yours, and he's got to take them as they come.'

This was bad! Unable to sit, I started to pace the floor. The other suppliants looked at me askance, as well they might.

Presently a buzzer alerted the secretary and she motioned to the next-in-line whom I recognized as one of the Goldmark directors. He went in.

Loud words began to emerge. Finally they ceased, and the director came out, crestfallen.

He had got half-way out when Goldmark himself loomed up, framed in the doorway of his private sanctum.

'Hey, Harry!' said Goldmark, 'tell those extra people on your ballroom set that no woman over twenty-five is to appear in evening gowns.'

'And what would they wear at a Court ball, in that case?' the director asked.

'Something respectable,' answered Goldmark. 'No indecent exposure, except on the young.'

The director turned on his heel and started to leave.

'Wait a minute!' called Goldmark. 'Tell the guy you got playing Disraeli to take that monocle out of his eye. What we're striving for in motion pictures is simplicity.'

The director flared up. 'Do you want this picture to be historically correct, Mr Goldmark,' he inquired—'or do you not?'

'Not if it's bad for the box office,' said Goldmark. 'A monocle may be historically correct, but it makes the guy look like a gigolo. And the public would think the Queen's got him hanging around for no good reason!'

The director strode the remaining steps to the outer door, then turned and said: 'You'll have to get somebody else to finish this picture. I quit!'

Goldmark was clearly set aback. 'Oh now Harry,' he pleaded, going over to smooth the man's coat lapel. 'Come on back and leave us talk things over.'

'Mr Goldmark,' the director answered, 'the act of talking presupposes that one first knows a language.' And he went out, slamming the door in the face of his superior.

Goldmark appeared harassed and I was myself perturbed. It all boded so badly for my interview. Goldmark stood a moment, then he turned to his secretary and said:

'Go tell Sidney he should quick shove another director on that ballroom set before the overhead eats us up!'

Sighing, he started back to his inner sanctum and at that moment he noted me.

'Well!' he said. 'And what are *you* here for?'

'Mr Goldmark!' I exclaimed. 'I am here on an errand of gravest urgency.'

'What's up now?' he asked.

'Something for private consultation,' I answered, quietly adding that the matter was in the way of being unthinkable.

'So!' he exclaimed. 'You think you can show me something in the way of troubles that ain't been thought up yet? For a young fellow, you got confidence!'

Then he opened the door leading to his private office and gestured me to enter.

'Go on in!' he said, 'and listen while I interview a few of these other rabble rousers. And if you can top what you've heard by the time it comes your turn, you're a guy that ought to belong in the motion-picture business!'

With a long-drawn-out sigh, he asked who was next. An apprehensive-looking chap jumped up and strode into the inner sanctum with us. Goldmark motioned me to a seat in a far corner, and the chap was given a chair facing the desk.

'Charlie,' began Goldmark, with an outward show of calm which I felt to be backed by a whole world of inner menace, 'the reason I sent for you is because I got to know what's going on in the scenario department.'

'Everything is going on very well, Mr Goldmark,' answered Charlie, 'especially since we got Owens on from New York.'

'So that's what *you* think, is it?'

Charlie appeared frightened, and said nothing.

'Well, then,' continued Goldmark, 'let *me* tell *you* what's going on in *your own* department!'

Striding over to Charlie, he shook a finger in the poor chap's face. 'From the minute you brought that expert on technique here from New York, do you know what's happened?'

'I'm not sure what you're trying to get at, Mr Goldmark.'

'Well then, I'll tell you,' said Goldmark. 'The guy goes through the files in the script department and starts looking for holes in our scenario plots. Then he goes to work, stuffing them full of what he calls 'reasonable motivation.' And he straightens out every plot we own, in a couple of weeks. The outcome is, there ain't nothing left for anyone else in the whole department to do. *And what's the result?'*

Goldmark paused a moment for effect, before continuing.

'I'll tell you what it is!' he then thundered. 'With nothing for her to do now in the scenario department, my sister Reba goes out joyriding and smashes up her brand new roadster before she's got insurance on it. Her two daughters, my nieces, with no plot problems to puzzle out, get into even worse mischief hanging around cowboys on motion-picture sets! My brother's boy, just because he's got no scenario structures to construct, goes yachting and gets arrested at Redondo Harbour, with a keg of Mexican beer on board! *And all because you import from New York a guy that does their work for them!'*

Now Goldmark's voice rose even higher. 'If they had ever bothered to learn a trade, it would be different,' he screamed. 'But the ignorant know-nothings can't be anything *but writers*! And if I wasn't such a fond-hearted brother, uncle, and cousin that I keep em on the payroll, even while they're loafing, this guy Owens would be taking the bread and butter out of the mouths of four innocent people.'

'I'm sorry, Mr Goldmark,' said Charlie, with, I felt, a tone of resignation. 'What do you want me to do?'

'Send that guy Owens back to Broadway, where he can construct indestructible motivation to his heart's content, without breaking up the morale of the whole motion-picture industry.

'There's nothing wrong with the motion-picture industry,' said Goldmark, his face livid with rage, 'that a dearth of good pictures can't cure.'

The secretary entered at this point, saving Charlie further grief. He bowed acquiescence to his chief and made a humble exit.

'Mr Seligman's here,' the secretary announced.

'Tell him to wait for his turn.'

'But Mr Goldmark,' she replied, 'it was you who sent for him!'

It was at this juncture Seligman entered. A soft-spoken young man, he was the first individual that morning to greet Goldmark with a tone of matching authority.

'Sit down, Bernie,' said Goldmark, conducting him personally to a seat. 'What's this I hear about your going to quit the studio?'

Seligman smiled. 'I guess that's about right,' he replied.

A moment followed during which Goldmark seemed to be on the brink of tears. And then he turned to me.

'Bliss, here's a young fellow I give his first start in pictures. And now he quits me cold!'

'You could have offered me a partnership,' spoke up Seligman.

'It ain't too late to talk it over yet, is it?' Goldmark asked, brightening up.

'I'm afraid it is,' the young man answered. 'I'm joining Stein's organization. I'm going to marry his daughter.'

Goldmark seemed to crumple. Staring straight into space, he said nothing for a moment. Then, when able again to articulate, he cried:

'Can you beat it? With all the marriable nieces, cousins, aunts and what nots I got right here on the lot, they let Herman Stein's girl walk off with the catch of the season.'

A tone of genuine affection came into Goldmark's voice as he went over to caress the youth's shoulder.

'Want to know something, Bliss?' he asked, 'this young fella's been smart enough to gyp me out of a cool million while he's been working for me. I couldn't be fonder of him if he belonged among my own nephews, cousins, uncles, and son-in-laws. And now he'll be working against me in a rival organization!'

Seligman shrugged, rose, walked to the door, turned, and said: 'I'll see you tonight at the poker game.' Then he went out.

Looking at the clock, I noted it was almost time for C. C. and the boys to arrive, and I felt a desperate need to brief Goldmark on our errand.

I arose. 'I hate to be importunate, Mr Goldmark,' I said, 'but this matter of mine concerns Viola Lake.'

Goldmark began to show signs of listening to me. 'Viola Lake!' he muttered. He reached for the button and buzzed. 'Viola Lake! There's another thorn in the side of Goldmark Pictures! America's Favourite Film

Flopper gets herself messed up in a murder case. That diary they found will be read in open court—and the public's going to find out she's been caught necking!'

'If "necking" were only all!' thought I. The secretary entered.

'Go get me my nephew,' ordered Goldmark. 'Which one?' asked the secretary.

'The one that calls himself Laurence St Vincent.'

The secretary left and once more Goldmark turned to me. 'Now!' he exclaimed. 'If you think you've brought me bad news about Viola Lake, just listen to the bad news I got to tell you!' He picked up a legal document. 'Do you know what *this* is?' he asked. He shook it at me, as if I were guilty of having drawn it up. 'It's Viola Lake's contract! Yesterday I decided that in spite of the fact I've spent a million on her publicity, it's cheaper to get rid of Viola, if she's going to be smeared up in a scandal. So I sent to the legal department for her contract.'

Red fury diffused his visage.

'Do you know what I find out?' he screamed. 'I find out that the identical nephew I made the head of my legal department was romancing Viola Lake at the time we signed her! And in order that nothing don't interfere with his romance, he sneaks the morality clause out of her contract…the clause that is the only known means in existence to get rid of her. And he makes me, his innocent uncle, sign it!'

Goldmark leaped from his chair. *'As a result,'* he screamed—full into my face, 'no matter what happens, I've got Viola Lake on my hands for the next five years, on a sliding scale, going upward! If anybody was to ask

me which way I got more troubles—as president of
Goldmark Films or as an uncle to nephews and
nieces—I wouldn't know how to answer!'

He started to pace the floor in agony.

'In the early days of France,' he cried, 'they had the
guillotine! I wish I had one now, in the place of the
movietone...If Viola Lake does something illegal—like
murder orphans or *take dope*—I couldn't get rid of her!'

'Take dope!' My heart stood still.

At this point the secretary entered and said: 'Mr St
Vincent is out playing polo.'

This was the last straw.

'So!' exclaimed Goldmark. 'He gets too lazy for golf
and has to chase balls on *horseback*! When he comes in,
tell him for me he's fired!'

'Yes, Mr Goldmark,' said the secretary. Then she
added: 'Mr Cahoon is outside with two gentlemen from
the Hollywood Boulevard Association.'

'I took the liberty of sending for them,' I spoke up,
'because what I have to report to you, Mr Goldmark, is
so far-reaching in its reverberation that our city itself
has got to take cognizance of it!'

For the first time that morning Goldmark appeared
to take my plea seriously. 'Well,' he said, 'do you want
those knobheads to come in?'

'I think it wise,' I replied, truly thanking Heaven in
my relief at having friendly faces near when I should
break the news about Viola.

C. C. Cahoon entered, followed by Milton Purdy and
Ray Beacom of the Hollywood Boulevard Association.
And, with my morale stiffened by the presence of the
boys, I faced the roomful.

'Gentlemen,' I said, 'last evening I was with Viola Lake.'

Goldmark groaned.

'I got her confidence, gentlemen,' I continued, 'and she acquainted me with the probable contents of the Geiger diary.' I paused. They were all attention. 'Indubitably the volume contains records of Miss Lake's association with various admirers. But it may also reveal to the world the fact that she has been in the habit of taking a certain chemical aid to vivacity.'

A deep hush followed my statement.

Finally Goldmark turned to C. C. Cahoon and asked: 'What's he trying to say?'

C. C. coughed uncomfortably. 'If I understand right,' he said, 'it involves a matter of drug addiction.'

Goldmark's face took on an expression which I had only seen duplicated in photographs of Mussolini in the throes of anger. He turned to me, unable to utter a sound, but his eyes shot a stupefied query as to whether this was true. Closing my own eyes, I merely nodded. Then only, did Goldmark start to crumple.

'What a morning!' he wept. 'A ballroom set with fifteen hundred extras is going to run into overtime, because a lot of old women past twenty-five have got to go and cover their cleavage...my scenario department throws nieces and nephews into complications that are even more complicated than the plots they work on...a guy I taught my most confidential underhand tricks to takes 'em to a rival organization...I got Viola Lake under contract for the next five years, no matter how many morality clauses she breaks, and now I find out she's got herself addicted. If I had any hair, I'd tear it!'

Goldmark, with an expression like Mussolini's in the throes of anger, cried, 'What a morning…if I had any hair, I'd tear it!'

A poignant silence followed. Purposely I allowed that silence to sink in. For I wished my next words to have their proper import.

'Mr Goldmark and gentlemen,' I said simply, 'I have a plan.'

C. C. and the boys from the HBA evinced attention. But Goldmark, with a look that was rather darkly dyed with doubt, asked:

'Yes? Well? For instance?'

'My plan,' I went on, 'is this: The opening of the Barco trial is set for next week, and from its very beginning, the good name of Hollywood is going to cry out for protection. That protection will be a scattered misdirected mess, unless some one man is put in charge, whose love for Hollywood is proven. In other words, gentlemen,' I went on, 'what the Barco case needs is a Czar! Someone who will be approved by the Hollywood Chamber of Commerce, the Hollywood Boulevard Association, and the Motion Picture Academy of Arts and Sciences. Someone who will protect the case as Will Hays protects the motion-picture industry, Judge Landis the national sport of baseball, and Al Smith the theatrical interests in New York.'

'Bravo, Bliss!' cried out C. C. Then, turning to the others, he exclaimed: 'Boys, I believe he's struck a solution!'

'Oh, you do?' spoke up Goldmark. 'Over in the old country, *one* Czar was too many. And in a democratical government like America, we already got three. And you want to add on another! And that's a solution?'

'Now, wait a moment, Mr Goldmark,' spoke up C. C. 'I believe that the Bliss Plan is entirely feasible—and more especially so if Elmer will undertake the Czarship himself.'

'Hear! Hear!' cried the boys from the HBA. But Goldmark shot a dark glance in my direction.

'So!' he said. 'A guy murders seven perfectly harmless morons and it comes out during the trial that America's Favourite Film Flopper is a hop-head! And you're going to give it an optimistical viewpoint?'

'Mr Goldmark,' I exclaimed, somewhat in exasperation. 'I have not offered this solution without having carefully thought the matter over. Distressing as were the seven Barco murders, I found cheering facts interspersed among them.'

'Oh, yes?' inquired Goldmark. 'For instance?'

'Does it not seem fortuitous,' I asked, 'that Barco invariably married his victims!'

C. C. and the boys from the HBA shared my satisfaction about this point, but Goldmark still remained stubbornly unconvinced.

'So you think that's a selling point for murder, do you?' he asked.

And, to be perfectly fair, there was a reason perhaps for his opposition. For the Czarships of that era were merely the beginning of a profession which, today, spreads the entire length of Madison Avenue in New York, glamorizing murder, via TV, and whetting the public appetite for it. However, that day I held my ground.

'Does it mean nothing to you,' I argued, 'that Barco's wives went to their deaths unsullied?'

'Well,' admitted Goldmark, 'maybe that *is* a box-office angle.'

'An angle,' I exclaimed, 'which I can emphasize in every word I write about the whole distasteful business!'

Goldmark shrugged. 'Who knows,' he finally conceded, 'perhaps a shmohawk like you is what the situation requires.'

I thanked him and went on. 'The second part of my scheme,' I said, 'would be to start *immediately* on what I shall call a "prophylactic" campaign for Miss Lake, in order to ease the blow to the public if the worst should happen. A campaign describing her as a homebody; going into her more conventional activities.'

This seemed to throw Goldmark into fresh dejection. I heard him mutter to himself: 'Homebody ...*Viola?*' Then, aloud, he added: 'Young fellow, there's one difficulty I bet you ain't thought up yet!'

'And that is?' I queried.

'If we're going to exhibit Viola Lake as a homebody you'll have to personally police the job *yourself*, and make certain she stays home.'

This was an eventuality of which, indeed, I had not thought. However, I hesitated but a brief moment and then (with a mental reservation that I would enlist Mother's chaperonage) I agreed.

'You can count on me,' I declared. 'I'll take Viola under surveillance immediately.'

'In that case,' said Goldmark, 'and seeing there ain't no other way out, I give in.'

It was at this point that C. C. Cahoon, in response to an expression of doubt still lingering on Goldmark's countenance, arose and put his hand on my shoulder. 'Mr Goldmark,' said C. C., 'Hollywood is luckier in the possession of Elmer than I believe you realize!' He then went into a eulogy on my poor self; to wit, that up to the present moment, my only date had been my mother.

For a moment Goldmark looked at me incredulously and then, in his crude way, he questioned me about a certain intimate fact of my personal life. I was able, looking him squarely in the eye, to answer Goldmark in the affirmative.

'So the Mamma is the only sweetheart!' said he, dumbfounded. I nodded a proud assent.

Well, Goldmark remained in his state of daze until the conference was finally brought to a close with the decision that the Czar of the Barco case would be my humble self.

Congratulations followed and I started to leave, along with C. C. and the boys from the HBA, when Goldmark called me back for a private word.

'Now, young fella,' he said in tones of kindly warning. 'I hope you realize that as Czar of the Barco case, you got to keep yourself strictly unassaultable.'

Smiling over his grammatical lapse, I assured Goldmark that indeed I did.

'Well,' he said, after a moment's speculation and a sigh, 'with Viola Lake on your hands, I hope you ain't bit off no more than you can chew.'

Six

The Day a Star Blushed

THE FOLLOWING DAY I launched into my 'prophylactic' campaign for Viola, confident over its outcome. I started it off by penning an item for my column.

'We are all aware,' I wrote, 'that Viola Lake is the essence of carefree youth. And I presume a great many of her public believe she is nothing more. I myself happen to know better. I have had a peep behind the façade of that seemingly carefree little character, and I have discovered that Viola Lake holds in her heart an Ideal—that she loves wild things...that she appreciates the song of birds, the hum of bees...recognizes the beauty of high mountains, and bows to the ineffable loveliness of leaf and blade and petal.'

This I felt to be true in essence, even though I wrote it at a time when our acquaintance had consisted of but two meetings—only one of which had actually been *en tête-à-tête*. This was all to be changed now, and I was to try and pilot Viola's frail craft out of the Sargasso Sea of careless impulse in which it had cruised (without a compass), into the calm waters of quiet social intercourse. But, by this same token, I was to be put to a certain test—placed in daily contact with a young lady who had shown, during the one evening I spent alone with her, a marked predilection for myself.

Now, it may seem strange that aside from my one involvement with Viola in a hammock, I had never been this near to any girl anywhere; even in Hollywood where more money is spent on peroxide, cosmetics, perfume, and gay lingerie than any city in the world (Paris included)... Hollywood, the very locale in which flavoured lipsticks were invented and may be obtained in pineapple, banana, lemon, lime, wild cherry, raspberry, or in fact, any of the berry flavours, according to taste.

I had small fear of succumbing to the charms of little Miss Lake! Oh, no! I know myself too well for that. And, mind you, I did not consider myself at all unique. I believed that even in Hollywood there were many young men like me, who could find themselves in the presence of a beautiful girl without any thought of evil entering their minds; or who, if such a thought should arise, would hesitate to bring the matter up, out of fear of what it might lead to—clean-cut chaps who make America what it is today, in Hollywood, just as in Kansas City, Detroit, Akron, Ohio, or Galveston, Texas.

As soon as I had mapped out a course of conduct for Viola, I repaired to the Goldmark studio to take up my activities as the little star's 'watch-dog,' so to speak. On that occasion, Goldmark himself took on the duty of leading me to the sound-stage where she was working.

On our progress through the broad studio lot, we passed several film celebrities of world renown, who looked my way and smiled and nodded. I was unaware whether the news of my appointment had as yet leaked out or not. 'Do you know,' thought I, 'that I am Czar?'

We reached Viola's set, which I found to represent the dormitory of a select girls' boarding school. Viola, garbed in red satin pyjamas, was in the midst of a scene where she was caught by an outraged schoolmarm in the act of entertaining a bevy of sailors.

Watching the progress of the scene, I was now to learn that the studio had set itself the task, for the first time in the history of the cinema, of photographing *in Technicolour* the actual process of a blush suffusing the female countenance.

The press department had been alerted and a campaign already mapped out which would announce to the entire United States: VIOLA BLUSHES!

Viola had been given every possible help to attain the necessary climax. The scene had been specially written to provoke embarrassment and in order not to impede the colour process, she wore no make-up. It appeared, however, that the entire morning's efforts had failed to induce the required blush.

After we had witnessed several unsuccessful 'takes,' Goldmark spoke up and suggested a rewrite of the scene.

'How can you expect the U.S. Navy to embarrass an old hand like Viola?' he quipped.

A sardonic laugh greeted Goldmark's sally; one in which the director, cast, electricians, and prop-men all joined. Viola bit her lip. I really could have killed Goldmark for his cruel method of reproach. The poor child! To be made the butt of heartless wisecracks and have self-respect publicly stripped from her by the cruel snickers of associates.

Viola in a scene where she was caught by an outraged schoolmarm in the act of entertaining a bevy of sailors.

As one more 'take' was attempted, I happened to move into Viola's line of vision, and suddenly seeing me while she was the subject of all those nautical leers, caused a deep flush of embarrassment to suffuse Viola's countenance (matched, I must confess, by another one of mine).

'Shoot!' called the director quickly. And, in a trice, the scene was 'in the can'—an indisputable testimony to the fact that Viola was capable of blushing. But, by the same token, it was a premonition to everyone who witnessed the scene that Viola Lake and I had an effect on each other which tended to be incendiary. And I sensed that Goldmark was alarmed.

Now looking at his watch, the director noted it was the noon hour, and gave orders for the luncheon break. Goldmark, although obviously discommoded over the future relationship of his star and me, announced to Viola my appointment as Czar of the Barco case.

'Elmer's first job,' he told her, 'is to suggest a few occupations that will take the place of what you're doing now and at the same time be legal.'

I gave Viola a reassuring smile and her face brightened. 'Oh, how lovely!' she exclaimed.

'Take Elmer to lunch at your bungalow,' Goldmark continued. Then, addressing me, he added crudely: 'and watch out she doesn't maul you!' Again Viola bit her lip, and at the moment how I hated Goldmark!

Viola led me toward the bungalow which served as her home while at the studio, doing so with such friendly confidence that I felt more than ever incensed over Goldmark's left-handed indication that she might attempt my entanglement.

We entered the bungalow and she led me into an exotic sort of—well, shall I say, Oriental boudoir? The walls were hung in black satin, artistically picked up by

Viola made me comfy on a low velvet divan. Gazing into my face with wide-eyed confidence, she exclaimed, 'Now!'

brilliant tones of red. Viola insisted on making me 'comfy' among the myriad cushions of a low black velvet divan. (To tell the truth, I was anything but 'comfy,' but her intentions were so charmingly hospitable I did not like to reveal to the poor child that I preferred to be honestly sitting in an upright wooden chair.)

We had scarcely settled down, when she jumped up, announcing that the sun was too bright. So she pulled the blinds down and turned on the dim light of a small red hanging lantern; after which she stepped to a teak-wood table and lighted some Chinese incense in a burner. Then picking up a cushion, she plumped it on the floor, sank down beside me, and gazing into my face with wide-eyed confidence, exclaimed: '*Now!*'

Well, my enforced exploration into Viola's past ensued and as she proceeded to unfold it, I was to hear a truly pitiable tale—a tale not of the glamour of her screen career, but of the talent which had been required of her to posture prettily before a camera.

Finally the spoken word had made its appearance in Hollywood, and Viola was called upon to *memorize lines*. One day, in the midst of an important scene, something in the poor little brain went snap! Viola's mind became a blank and work had to be postponed to the next day.

That evening, she allowed a chance acquaintance she had picked up at a gas station to argue her into attending a party in the hope it might revive her spirits. The function had started innocuously enough, with merely some gay clowning on the part of those present, but Viola's fatigue had increased, so she asked her hostess for an aspirin tablet. The hostess had gone out and returned with a little box full of pills. Viola inquired what they might be.

'They're something that's a lot better for you girls than the medicine you're always taking,' was the hostess's reply. So Viola did not hesitate to do as she was bidden. As a result of that medicament, her spirits rose as if by magic. And next day, on repeating the experiment with pills presented by her 'generous' hostess, Viola *had remembered every line she was required to repeat*. But from that moment was the die cast. She must either stop trying to act, or continue to rely on an artificial jog to memory.

Tears flooded Viola's eyes as she finished telling her story. And then, reaching into her bosom, she brought forth a crumpled newspaper clipping.

'Do you know what this is?' she asked and without waiting for an answer, continued: 'It's the publicity plug you wrote about me, Elmer! And, oh, *you don't know what it's done*. Nobody before ever realized that I loved mountains and birds and bees and flowers! Why, I never even knew it myself, *until you told me!* But now I have something definite to take the place of pills. I can give them up for ever, right away, at once—*today!*'

This was good news indeed, for I had feared that the habit in Viola was established. I cannot describe what a relief it was to hear the contrary from her own lips.

'My dear, dear child,' said I, 'you can count on me to lead you to locales where birds and bees and flowers abound and also to point out the mountains.'

She grasped my hand and raised it to her lips.

At this juncture Viola's gracious maid entered with a tray of chili con carne and I, sensing that the girl might misconstrue our mood, withdrew my hand and rose. It was apparent that the maid intended to remain and serve us, but Viola dismissed her, sending her off to the San Fernando Valley on an errand.

A trace ill at ease with emotion and as a means of doing something, I suggested we sit down to the table and feed the inner man. But Viola, disregarding the chili, continued to gaze at me. Well, this would never do! Realizing it might be well to broach the matter of her preoccupation with the opposite sex, I steered the conversation into that particular channel.

'Viola,' I said earnestly, 'I want you to give me your word of honour that in the future you will keep your name high above the possibility of smirch! Hold yourself sacred and when you feel that the interest of a suppliant is merely in your frail beauty and *not* in your moral attributes, shun him as you might a plague!'

'Oh, I will, Elmer!' she cried and sinking to her knees at my feet, she buried her head in my lap as a gesture of repentance and contrition.

A strange new exaltation swept over me and I don't know how long I might thus have remained, shaken by the depth of her atonement, had I not been suddenly startled by Goldmark's voice from the hallway, calling: 'Hey, what's going on in there?'

Realizing that the crass mind of Goldmark would never understand the innocence of our juxtaposition, I quickly removed the dainty burden from my lap. Then I rose to open the blinds and summon in God's sunshine.

Goldmark entered and stopped short. He looked at Viola and then at myself, after which his gaze travelled to the incense burner. And such is the power of evil suggestion, that I actually found myself blushing.

'W-e-l-l,' asked Goldmark, 'what's the score?'

I cleared my throat. 'Mr Goldmark,' I said, 'Viola has given me her word of honour to turn over a new leaf.'

And now Viola, noting from Goldmark's attitude that he seemed to require some sort of proof of good intent, reached into the pocket of her pyjamas, took out a pill box, went over to the open window, and threw it far out into her patio.

'*There, Mr Goldmark!*' she cried.

Still was Goldmark sceptical. 'You better try knocking off a little bit at a time,' he said dryly, 'until you get yourself down to a maximum.'

He now turned to me. 'What else is on your programme?'

'Just this, Mr Goldmark,' I said. 'Viola, at the present time, is living alone except for hired help. She ought to have a chaperon.'

At long last his face brightened. 'Now, that's an idea!' he exclaimed.

I turned to Viola and asked: 'Viola, would you consent to our sending for your nearest living relative, to introduce a touch of family life into your home?'

Viola hesitated a moment, then braced herself and said: 'I'll do anything you tell me, Elmer.'

'Ah!' I exclaimed, and turned to Goldmark as if to say: 'There! you see?'

'Okay,' said Goldmark. 'Who's your nearest relation?'

'It's Leroy Jones,' said Viola, 'a chiropodist in Kansas City. He's my husband.'

The news fell on us like a bombshell, for not even Goldmark was aware that Viola had ever stood before the marriage altar.

Slumping into his chair, Goldmark gave me one long look. 'That's a *fine* idea!' he said. 'America's Favourite Film Flopper *married* to a foot doctor!'

Realizing her frank revelation had been ill-taken, Viola tried to rectify matters by telling us it had merely been a marriage of convenience.

'Haven't you a feminine relation of some sort, Viola?' I inquired. 'Don't you have a *Mother?*'

'Of course I had—once,' she replied, a wistful tear lurking on her long curled eyelashes. 'But you see, Mamma and Papa lived in a trailer and one day soon after I was born, Mamma stepped on the gas and left us.'

'In polite terms, she was a tramp!' said Goldmark. 'And what about the Papa?'

Viola ignored his sarcastic tone. 'I guess I got on Papa's nerves,' she said, 'because he left soon after Mamma did. He never seemed to be a baby's man.'

Poor little thing, thought I, all alone in the world, without a soul to turn to in an hour of need.

'What other bums have you got in the family?' queried Goldmark.

'Papa's sister,' Viola spoke up, helpfully.

'Excellent!' I exclaimed.

'Well,' queried Goldmark, 'what's her name and police record?'

'Oh, Mr Goldmark!' cried the poor child, hurt. 'She's my Auntie Minnie and she's never been in jail in her whole life!'

This sounded encouraging, and even Goldmark appeared to cheer up a jot.

'All right!' he remarked, 'we'll send for her.'

I sat at the desk and asked for her aunt's name and the address.

'It's Miss Minnie Kinko,' she ventured, and added the address which was in Manitoba.

'Kinko!' Goldmark mused. 'And she's your father's sister?' Viola nodded. 'So,' he pursued relentlessly, 'for a real name you've got a name like *Kinko?*' Again Viola nodded. Goldmark gave me a bitter look. 'And *you* want to drag the Auntie clear from Manitoba in order to let the whole world know it!'

I felt myself perilously approaching impatience. 'After all, Mr Goldmark,' I said, 'what's in a name? The entire world has worshipped at the feet of idols who were christened Gladys Smith, Frances Gumm, Lillian Bohny, Freddy Bichel, Doug Uhlman, and Arlington Brugh. Why not let it also know that Viola Lake's real name is—'

Turning to Viola, I asked: 'What is it?'

'Ruby Kinko!' she faltered.

Goldmark shook his head in despair. I faced him.

'Now look here, Mr Goldmark, as a name, Ruby Kinko may not be distinguished, but at the same time it sounds *real* and *honest*. There's a note of sound security about it which I like. Moreover,' I went on, 'if we publicize the fact that Viola's father was a Kinko, the Public will feel that he must actually have existed and that we are not merely trumping up a father for Viola.'

Goldmark gazed at me, amazed at my ability to discover behind any cloud, a splotch of silver lining. 'Well,' he said finally, 'I give in. Send for Auntie Minnie. Things couldn't be worse, whatever happens!'

The upshot was that I penned a telegram to Miss Kinko to come at once.

Goldmark now suggested that Viola and I separate for the moment. I agreed to accompany him to his office. On the way there I tried to dispel his gloom. 'Cheer up, Mr Goldmark,' said I. 'Think how much has been accomplished in one day only! Why, I personally am delighted.'

Goldmark grunted and then he suddenly stopped short. 'Seeing you got the job to protect the good reputation of Hollywood,' he said, 'you better go pick up that box of stuff she threw out of the window. Some of them child actors might get hold of it and they're advanced enough already!'

Seven

Could Hollywood be Heaven?

THE OPENING DAY of the Barco trial broke over a Hollywood that was, as usual, sunny.

I arrived at the courtroom bright and early, and tasted for the first time the deference which the Czarship was to bring me. A special desk and chair had been arranged for me, and I was told to ask freely for any amount of assistance I desired from the polite courtroom attendants.

Then, quite naturally, I had to pose for photographs for the newspapers.

By a quarter to ten the courtroom began to fill up. It seemed as if half of our community was filing in.

Hollywood's arch enemy, Lansing Marshall, arrived, ready to put the worst possible face on the Barco murders, with results which would be detrimental to Hollywood in the extreme. The sight of him steeled me to do my own best to protect our city's name.

Mother came in and was courteously shown to a chair in the section specially reserved for ladies and, when I went to greet her, it naturally caused some little flurry of interest.

Then the newspaper boys, as I had feared, insisted

that Mother and I be photographed together. While we were looking about for some sort of an artistic background, I was surprised to see Viola entering court. I had warned her not to come near the trial until called as a witness, for I wished to prepare an entrance for her which would provide shock impact. And now, because I didn't particularly want to be seen with the little star in public (lest any predilection for her on my part be noted) I made my way to her side and demanded quietly: 'What are you doing here?'

'Oh, Elmer,' she said, 'Auntie Minnie *would* come to the trial, and I don't dare let her out alone!'

'But why not?' I asked.

'Because when I let her out yesterday she went down to Hollywood Boulevard and got her hair bleached.'

'What!' I cried.

Her face suffused with concern, Viola nodded. 'Elmer,' she said, 'I'm afraid we're going to have trouble with Auntie Minnie.'

At this juncture, Aunt Minnie entered, after having loitered in the corridor to collect autographs. A bright little old lady with dancing brown eyes, she bobbed into the room, her new 'Mary Pickford' coiffure providing an incongruous, not to say disturbing, note— considering her duties as a chaperon.

I preferred not to meet Miss Kinko at the moment, but the old lady felt otherwise. Heartily grabbing my hand, she cried out that she didn't *need* an introduction to 'Elmer,' for Viola talked of nothing else.

It was at this moment that Mother barged into the situation with a crisp: 'Elmer! Come with me!'

Not recognizing the snub, Miss Kinko spoke a

cheery word of greeting. Mother stiffened. Viola cast me a look of such pathetic appeal that I began to say a word of encouragement, when Mother jerked me away.

'I hope you'll see no more of that girl than your duties require!' said Mother vehemently.

Now I had felt this attitude of Mother's accumulating, but unexpressed, ever since she had first heard details of Viola's past. I scarcely knew how to combat it. Woman's inhumanity to woman is something which mere man has never yet found means to mitigate.

We reached the yard where the camera boys were waiting. But while they were trying to figure out something new in the way of mother-and-son poses, Mother's invective continued.

'That woman will never make a fool of me, no matter what she does to you!' said Mother. Not wishing the Press to suspect that any sort of personal relationship existed betwixt Viola and the Czar, I tried to quiet Mother.

'Oh, Elmer, shut up!' was Mother's crisp retort, as the boys placed my head on her breast and we had to smile into the cameras.

They had scarcely ceased clicking, when a court attendant rushed breathlessly into the yard and called out: 'Hurry up, Mr Bliss. Judge Olah is entering court!'

We rushed back into the courtroom, arriving just as the judge took his seat and rapped for order.

The Barco case was open!

My attention was now drawn to the defendant, Cal Barco. He was seated at a table with his attorneys, and I was struck with the surprisingly mild and inoffensive appearance of this murderer of seven women! Indeed,

Cal Barco with his attorneys. I was struck by the mild, inoffensive appearance of this murderer of seven women.

the photographers, who had previously posed him with various of the weapons he had used, found his expressions so benign that some of the more sensational newspapers actually refused to use the pictures as detrimental to interest in the case.

The morning was spent in selecting a jury. It did not take long, for naturally each and every talesman called was more than anxious to get his or her share of the generous publicity of the case.

After luncheon, followed the first testimony which revealed that the offence ultimately leading to the arrest of Barco was, strangely enough, *not* murder, but the mere theft of an automobile rug.

On October 17, Barco, leaving the scene of his seventh murder (of Amelia Cannondale) at Santa Monica, had started to motor to Hollywood. It happened to be the noon hour, so he had stopped the murder car near the crowded corner of Hollywood Boulevard and Highland Avenue and descended to a drugstore for a refreshing California orange drink.

On starting back to his car, he noted the sports roadster of Miss Lillian Swan (the motion-picture star) parked by the curb, with an ermine lap robe tossed carelessly across the back seat. Barco walked furtively over to Miss Swan's roadster, picked up the robe, tossed it into his convertible, and started down the Boulevard.

Now, it may seem incredible that anyone could steal so large, bulky, and *white* an object as an ermine rug at high noontide on the busiest corner of one of the world's busiest thoroughfares, and that nobody had reported the act to the police. Yet such had been the case.

One witness actually stood at the hood of Miss Swan's car and watched the theft take place. This witness, an elderly man by the name of Hinkle, was called to the stand. And as he took his place, one began to sense, as one does at a trial, that his testimony was going to tend toward the amusing.

A quaint type was Hinkle, one of those wrinkled old fellows from the Middle West who come to Southern California in the evening of their days to expand in its life-giving sunshine. He was sworn in, and the prosecuting attorney asked him where he lived.

The old fellow thought a moment and then spoke up with a quaver. 'Mr Prosecuting Attorney,' he said, 'I don't believe I *am* alive. I think I've passed on and this is Paradise.'

The court was somewhat befuddled by the old boy's

statement. But the prosecuting attorney, a man of wit, was never long at a loss for words. 'That's a nice compliment to us as a community, Mr Hinkle,' he said.

A murmur of approbation now swept the court and Hinkle, encouraged by it, started to explain. 'Folks,' said he, 'two months ago I left Pin Hook, Indiana, in a blizzard. And when I got off the train in Los Angeles, the sunshine was so dazzling I had to squint, and the glare of them Los Angeles sidewalks was so bright I thought they must be paved with mother-of-pearl. Well, they seemed so much like what I'd always heard about Heaven, I actually thought I must 'a died in that blizzard back in Indiana.

'And when I was on my way up from the depot, the streetcar passed a sight I couldn't hardly believe. I nearly barked my shins getting off that car to take another look. And folks, do you know what it was?'

He paused for effect before continuing.

'It was a billboard that stretched the entire length of the block, advertising a movie called *The Hollywood Revue*. And it had twenty-four *actual, living, breathing* girls, all posed artistic in their underwear on the lettering!

'Well,' said Hinkle, 'I stayed for a long time, gazing at them beautiful girls hovering up above the street traffic like they was angels. But finally, a little thing in a pink lace shirt called down and asked me to toss her up a cigarette, so then I knew I must still be on terry firma.'

Laughter in the courtroom. Hinkle expanded, for he had us going and he knew it.

'By that time,' he chortled, 'I begun to be hungry, so I started looking for some place to get myself a snack.

And I finally discovered one of these here cafeterias over on Sunset Boulevard. But what I never found out until later was that a movie studio was just around the corner.

'Well, I went into the cafeteria and then I stopped. For blamed if it wasn't full of more beautiful girls than I had ever even dared to dream about back in Pin Hook, where we only had one that I ever knew and she was such a novelty she got a job in a circus. I stood there in a stupor, deciding that I *must* be in Heaven when the door opened and in walked Napoleon Boneypart! Well, I *knew* that he had died!'

Again a burst of laughter rose from the spectators.

'And then,' continued Hinkle pertly, 'I looked over at a table in a corner and I seen Abraham Lincoln having lunch with Clara Bow. And thinks I to myself, if anything *could* compensate honest Abe for the trials he had on earth, it would be Clara Bow. So I guess there ain't no doubt that this is Heaven.'

(More laughter)

'Well, folks,' Hinkle went on, 'when I finished my snack and stepped out on Sunset Boulevard, I got a shock that really floored me. Because blamed if I didn't see coming down the street, plain as day, robes, beards, and all, the Twelve Apostles!

'Then I begun to git kind of faint standing there, watching them laughing and talking, in two and threes. When I "came to" a little bit, I sort of wavered into the corner drugstore to ask for a drink of water.

'And then I got another shock! For sitting there at the soda fountain, plain as any picture I ever seen of her, and all covered with jewels, was the Magdalen, having a chocolate malted. And while I'm standing there gasping, the Twelve Apostles all trooped in and joined her for a coke.

'Of course, in due time, I find out that they was only actor folks taking part in the Passion Play that's responsible for the spread of the living Gospel in Hollywood and takes place in a big outdoor theatre they built up in a gully. But I don't mind telling you that the first sight of them was a terrible shock to a fellow in my state of mind!

'I was still more or less shaky by nighttime, when I wandered on to Hollywood Boulevard to see what I could see. And I came to a glittering building that's got more different kinds of architecture on it than any I ever seen in all my life, and I've been to Coney Island! I thought it must be the Pearly Gate itself, but I found out it was only one of Grauman' s movie palaces. So I

Coming down Sunset Boulevard were the Twelve Apostles

bought myself a ticket for twenty-five cents and I went in the lobby.

'And blamed if the lobby hasn't got even more architecture than the outside. Gorgeous Assyrian lions is standing on Queen Anne pedestals, with that famous World War motto carved over their heads—"They Shall Not Pass." Why it just jerks you clear through Art and History, in one clip.

'I was standing there in a daze, when some other customers came up behind me and pushed me into the theatre. And while I'm trying to get my bearings in the dark, the most beautiful blonde I ever saw floats up to me, dressed in a grass skirt, like a Hula Hula dancer, with an electric bulb concealed in her bosom that throws a spotlight smack into her beautiful face. And blamed if she don't say: "Follow me!" So I *followed!* (Laughter.) It turned out that this Hawaiian blonde was

robes, beards and all.

an usherette, so I didn't get no further with her than a seat in the gallery.

'Well,' continued Hinkle, 'the movie that night was about father love, which is just as beautiful as mother love, if you know how to tackle it, with plenty of hard times and Sonny Boy sick as a pup, without hardly no chance to pull through. However, it ended happy at last. But when I got up to go out, I felt kind of dizzy.

'I staggered up the aisle and drifted into a place I found later was only the gents' room. But I didn't realize it then, because I'd been used to the kind we have in Pin Hook; and this here place was all pink satin clouds with angels flying around on the ceiling. The furniture was solid gold, and the ash trays was pure white alabaster.

'And then, folks, I had to rub my eyes and look twice, for blamed if the privy wasn't mother-of-pearl! "That settles it," said I. "*This is Heaven!*"'

Applause followed the quaint old fellow's tribute to Southern California and the judge felt some sort of official recognition was called for. He rose, awaited a lull, and said:

'I feel that Mr Hinkle ought to be commended officially on his testimony.'

Hinkle, now a little puffed up over the honours heaped on him, started off on a speech of thanks to the court. But the judge rapped for order and directed the prosecuting attorney to get down to Hecuba and proceed with the case.

The prosecuting attorney now addressed the witness:

'Mr Hinkle, you watched the defendant, Cal Barco, steal an ermine robe worth five thousand dollars out of Miss Swan's sports roadster?'

'Yes, sir, I did,' admitted Hinkle.

'And you did nothing about it?' asked the prosecuting attorney.

'No, sir,' answered Hinkle.

'And yet,' pursued the prosecuting attorney, 'you must have known that the auto belonged to Miss Swan, as it has her name, address and telephone number painted on the door.'

'Yes, sir,' murmured Hinkle.

'Now,' said the prosecuting attorney, 'can you explain to the court your negligence in not reporting this theft?'

For a moment Hinkle remained silent as if in a daze. Then he squared his shoulders and launched into a defence of his actions.

'Mr Prosecuting Attorney,' he began, 'I'll tell you why I didn't pay much attention when I seen that auto rug get stolen! I'd been standing there on the corner of Hollywood Boulevard and Highland Avenue for about an hour, watching the sights go by. The first thing that struck me was seeing two automobile trucks speeding down the boulevard at a good clip, with a sawed-off half of a fair-sized furnished house on each one of them! And it was sort of flabbergasting.

'Why, when we move a house in Indiana, we do it in one piece, and it ain't no fun! But this here family was *inside* the house, giving themselves a going-away party while their home was being whisked along from Glendale to Venice. It fair staggered me.

'And I ain't no more than half recovered, when I see, coming down the street, a fellow who's the living spit of Mussolini. So I begin to look him over with interest, and then I begin to think I'm seeing double, because

91

another one suddenly appears. Then blamed if I don't look down Hollywood Boulevard and there's a whole string of Mussolinis coming down the street!

'Well, I think I've gone plum daffy, till a fellow that's standing nearby tells me some movie director that's making an Italian picture had ordered Central Casting to round up all their Mussolinis. But seeing 'em in droves is kind of bewildering just the same.

'Another thing that sort of dazed me was that the Mack Sennett Movie Company was in the middle of the street, taking pictures, with a cross-eyed traffic cop. And it causes me no end of confusion, 'cause I can't figure out which is the boney-fide accidents and which belongs in the movie they're shooting.

'And about this time all the famous film stars begin to arrive at the Embassy Club for lunch, and seeing so many familiar faces I've got used to on the screen, is like a ghost story in reverse with the ghosts coming to life before your very eyes.

'So, when I notice this here Mr Barco steal that ermine rug, it's lost its sense of proportion, so to speak, and I don't pay it a second thought. In Pin Hook I'd 'a' yelled for the sheriff. But in Hollywood a fellow feels that a thing like larceny is sort of humdrum.

'That's why I didn't tell the policeman on the corner. And anyway, I didn't know whether he was a policeman or only a movie actor, so I let the matter go! And that's the whole story from A to Z, Mr Prosecuting Attorney.'

A round of applause followed, during which I was extremely annoyed by Viola's Auntie Minnie standing on her chair and tossing Hinkle a rose. I began to sense that the chaperonage we had counted on was not going to be all that might be desired.

'Witness excused,' spoke up the D.A., and Hinkle left the stand to pose for the cameras.

By this time the old fellow's head had begun to swell, and he was 'acting all over the place,' as the saying goes. But finally I was tipped off that the newspaper boys were getting him to substitute for Barco in a series of murder attitudes with a fire axe. So I hurried out and stopped them—my first act as Czar being to prevent sensationalism entering the case. However, poor old Hinkle's disappointment was more than appeased when a scout for a big producer suddenly appeared and arranged with him for a picture test.

By this time the court had been adjourned for the day, with Miss Swan's chauffeur to be called to the stand the next morning.

As I started to accompany Mother home, I ventured a glance across to where Viola stood. She waved discreetly to me, but her expression spoke more freely of the security she felt in my championship. The incident evoked Mother's ire. She flounced me out of the courtroom.

'I want to warn you, Elmer, for your own good,' she declared, 'that's it's not going to be any help to this case for that disreputable blonde to be casting sheep's eyes at a Czar who could very easily fall from grace and crowd the seven murders of Cal Barco right out of the headlines!'

I did not like the implication. Could it be possible that the world at large would misunderstand, as Mother did, the pure relationship which was blossoming between Viola and myself?

Eight

Joy Rules the Night

DURING THE SECOND day of the trial, Justice began closing in on Barco. Called to the stand was the chauffeur of the sports car from which the lap robe had been thefted. The youth, by name Bert Mills, had been absent during the act of larceny, but when he returned to his car and noted the robe missing, he began an inquiry among bystanders and thus contacted Hinkle. The old fellow, galvanized into consciousness by Mills' concern, was then able to recall, that he *had* seen the larceny take place and that the perpetrator wore an extremely *heavy beard*. To Mills, this fact was clue enough to work on. Being an exceptionally quick-witted youth, he knew that in our community practically every beard of exceptional density is registered at the Central Casting Bureau for Motion Pictures. So he forthwith grabbed Hinkle by the hand and rushed him off there.

Now Central Casting is a unique institution, the like of which exists in no other city of the globe. For in Hollywood every soul within a radius of miles registers his or her photograph for extra work in films—some as a means of livelihood, others to pick up a bit of spending money, a few (such as teenage boys and girls) in a spirit of fun, still others (such as pampered society folk) out of boredom. But all of them are possessed of physical peculiarities which make them valuable as 'types.' There in the casting files, along with pictures of the world's largest collection of beautiful girls, are photographs of the world's largest collection of giants, dwarfs, twins, triplets, precocious kiddies, fat people, men with six fingers, human skeletons, aborigines from every quarter of the globe, physical doubles of Greta Garbo, and *men with beards!*

At the Bureau, Mills asked if he and Hinkle might look through the Beard files, and permission was granted.

The Beard files were bulky, for any number of our Hollywood citizenry find the growing of beards for the motion-picture industry as pleasant and easy a way to make a living as has ever been devised.

The two men skipped through the Short Beards, Oriental Beards, Vandyke Beards, Latin Quarter Beards, Assorted Medium Beards, General Grant Beards (any number of these), Hindu Beards, Abraham Lincoln Beards (a whole file of these alone), Gladstone Beards, Square-Cut French Beards, Apostle Beards (ah, they were getting into the longer beards at last!), High Priest Beards, Old Testament Beards, Divided Emperor Maximilian Beards, Pioneer Beards, Viking Beards, and finally Mormon Beards. It was among these that Hinkle identified a photograph of Barco! For it seems that Barco, fancying himself a ladies' man (and why not, after seven marriages?), had listed himself for Mormon Beard roles at the instigation of his fourth murder victim who had said: 'With your beard, dear, you ought to be in movies!'

Mills secured Barco's photograph from the gentleman in charge, rushed to the Hollywood police station to report the theft, and less than five minutes later, detectives with his picture in hand were on the trail of Cal Barco.

On their way, they stopped at every gas station along the main boulevards to question the attendants. Finally, at Ye Olde Gasse Filling Station on Avocado Avenue, they learned that their man, having paused to get oil for his car, had asked about the route to San Diego. They headed in that direction and, at San Juan Capistrano by-the-Sea came upon Barco sitting in the quaint old Spanish Mission Drive-in, eating a hot tamale. At the moment, Barco's back was to the road so he didn't see the detectives close in on his convertible which, in their quest for the stolen lap rug, they proceeded to search. The robe, however, was missing, for by that time Barco had disposed of it at a pawnshop in Glendale.

The detectives placed Barco under arrest and, without informing him of the nature of the charge, took him back to Hollywood for questioning.

Thus it was that Barco, apprehended for mere larceny, now began to suspect that one or another of his murders had been uncovered. During the return trip, Barco kept muttering to himself in meaningless phrases, such as: 'They're under sand dunes...They're better off, I tell...I saved their souls.' The detectives, commenting on Barco's behaviour, felt that he merely belonged among the myriad citizens of our community who are mentally unhinged—that he was a more or less harmless 'nut'!

However, while in his cell awaiting trial for theft,

Barco, in a fit of apprehension, made an attempt to take his own life. The attempt had failed because, when endeavouring to cut his wrists, this murderer of seven women had fainted at the sight of blood. The jail authorities—attaching no particular significance to the episode—offered Barco whisky to revive him; but the old fellow, a lifelong teetotaller, refused it, and no more was thought of the matter.

Then it was that District Attorney Welch entered the case. A man of vaulting ambition, with one eye on the mayorship of Los Angeles, nothing ever escaped him which might possibly lead to personal publicity.

It was reported to Welch's office that a thief in the city jail had attempted suicide. Welch wanted to know why. No one knew. Now Welch had a pet theory that everyone is guilty of breaking more laws than he ever gets caught at.

The suicide attempt looked to him like an opportunity to put his theory to the test. So he paid a call on Barco in his cell and began their chat by stating bluntly:

'Barco, we've got the goods on you! It'll be a lot better if you come clean.'

At first Barco was evasive and shifty. But with Welch's relentless pursuit of the subject, Barco finally 'broke' and started confessing to one murder after another. By the time Barco reached the count of three, the situation seemed to Welch almost too good to be true. But if true, it was the case of which he had dreamed, the case which would throw him into headlines all over America as the hero of a great murder trial.

Welch summoned jail officials to Barco's cell. But to

Welch's chagrin, the police captain pooh-poohed Welch's credulity in Barco's confession. Barco was clearly a 'nut.' It required strength, bravado, daring to commit murder. 'That worm a murderer? Ridiculous!' Then, for the first time since his arrest, a glint of spirit lit Barco's eyes. His manhood had been attacked. He stiffened and rose to his feet. He'd show them!

'Is that so?' he queried. 'Well, for ten years I've been murdering women. I can lead you to every one of the bodies, and there ain't four, nor five, nor six of 'em—there's *seven!*'

The next day the police captain, in derision, organized what he termed 'Welch's Wild Goose Chase.' For indeed it seemed incredible that anyone could go on committing murder for ten years and not get caught at it, even in Hollywood. The searching party consisted of the police captain, Welch, Barco, policemen with shovels, newspaper reporters, and cameramen.

Barco, his state of apprehension gone, never to return, had assumed a matter-of-factness which remained his principal attitude from that time on, He directed the cortege of autos to the sand dunes near Santa Monica. Stopping the cars at a fork in the road, he got out, paced off a certain distance to a spot between two shrub-covered sand hills, and indicated a location.

Orders were given to dig. Nothing was found. Welch was worried. The police captain chortled. The newspaper boys cracked jokes and again Barco's pride was aroused. With greater precision he again paced off a location, this time a little more to the left.

With quibs and gibes, the policemen again started

digging. Welch was on edge. The captain was remarking that it was a nice day for a picnic when finally one of the shovels struck an object.

'There's something here!' said the digger. Joking stopped and everyone gathered around. The digger, thrusting about with his shovel, now raised into view a package crudely wrapped in one of the murderer's Hollywood sport shirts. Although it was a mere fragment of the victim's remains, it was enough. Welch was wild with delight. His elation grew as Barco's seven disclosures brought to light one reward after another.

Now did Welch truly become the man of the hour, and everything that followed in the procedure of Justice was a new triumph for him. It went to his head, and his ambition increased.

It was apparent that Welch was in cahoots with Marshall and would use his power as D.A. to drag every possible sensation into the case. Every new scandal which would provide more 'copy' for Marshall's pen would thus mean more publicity for Welch.

I knew that both these cynics were waiting with impatience for the dramatic moment when Viola was called to the stand. Once there, the D.A. with devilish cleverness would provide Marshall with headlines: 'Viola's Multiple Romances'… Viola Lake an Addict'… 'Downfall of Another Film Idol!' It would be fine publicity for the man who was willing to walk to the mayor's throne over the broken reputation of a helpless girl!

I studied Welch closely as the trial progressed for any hint which might give me a lead as to how he might be thwarted. It wasn't long before I sensed that there was something deeper than overvaulting ambition back of his desire for Viola's destruction. He was bitter and resentful toward her, *personally* resentful. A dreadful fear entered my consciousness that perhaps he had entertained aspirations toward Viola's favours—or, even more serious perhaps, that he had attained a share of them and had then been superseded by some luckier chap. I did not rest until I had tracked the mystery down. Well, here it is.

One day over a year before, there had been a cocktail party in an apartment of a downtown hotel. Viola had been urged to attend, by telephone, and not knowing the host or the character of the party, she had gone. She arrived late and as she entered the party, noted that gentlemen seemed to be in the majority; the air was thick with smoke, empty bottles were in evidence, and several of the guests were somewhat the worse for liquor.

Naturally, Viola had no wish to remain, but she felt she couldn't leave so soon after her arrival, in all politeness to her host. And it so happened that adjacent to a couch on which she had taken refuge was a small table on which she noted a vase of red rosebuds; while projecting from beneath the couch were a pair of feet which, as Fate would have it, belonged to District Attorney Welch.

As Viola sat there, a playful impulse overcame her to remove the shoes and socks from the unidentified feet and, as a prank, insert rosebuds between the toes.

A little later the district attorney woke up, emerged from under the couch, looked at his watch, and realized he had an engagement that very hour to address a meeting of the Culture Forum on 'The Civic Spirit of the Southland,' in the Byzantine room of the hotel where his wife, as president of the forum, was to preside. He made his way to his host's bedroom where he carefully brushed himself off, neatly arranged his hair, and painstakingly selected his hat from the many on the bed. Then, noting neither the absence of his footwear nor the presence of the rosebuds, he made his way to the Byzantine room and, with his usual dignity, mounted the rostrum. The effect on the intellectuals among his audience may well be imagined.

The incident, aside from reflecting on Welch's political career, had all but wrecked his home life. He never rested until he discovered who the culprit was, and when he did, he vowed vengeance on Viola Lake if ever the chance came his way. *And here it was!* By such innocent actions are human tragedies sometimes set in motion.

During these first days of the trial I didn't have as much time to commiserate with Viola as I should have liked. In the first place, it was difficult for us to meet. We couldn't be seen together, for the tongue of Scandal was ever ready to link our names, and the tongue of Scandal finds but one thing to say of the association of a man with a girl, no matter how innocent. I couldn't invite Viola to our house, for Mother snobbishly refused to receive her.

Now the Czarship had not affected my own sense of social values, but Mother had attained a reflected glory through it, which had opened the doors of Los Angeles-Pasadena Society to her. There, Mother was received by the scions of aristocratic lines which are dominated by the Budweisers (of beer derivation), the Chalmers (of underwear origin), and the Heinzes (whose forebears founded a nationally famous trade in pickles). I hated being dragged into the salons of these aristocrats. But Mother insisted, for it is seldom indeed that anyone remotely connected with the cinema is ever received in their exclusive midsts. In fact, it was not until the King of Spain had visited at Pickfair that Mary and Doug were beckoned to cross the sacred barriers which separate Los Angeles and Pasadena from the *hoi polloi*.

Mother even went so far as to trump up for me matrimonial opportunities with Pasadena debs who had been educated abroad, and with those of the more lenient Los Angeles area where a debutante was a girl who had been to high school. But at long last came a time when I broke away from Mother and her society 'chi-chi' in order to spend a cosy evening with Viola and her chaperon at her home.

However, such a hotbed of gossip had grown up during the trial, that every precaution had to be taken to keep my visit from being whispered to the world, Society, and even, alas, to my own mother.

When I arrived at Viola's I was shown, to my surprise, into the *kitchen*. Viola greeted me, in checked apron, ladle in hand, and explained it was the cook's night out and that she herself was preparing dinner.

I sat and watched proceedings. There was to be roast chicken with dressing, giblet gravy, asparagus, new peas with a sprig of mint, creamed onions, and mashed potatoes—all chosen, prepared, and cooked by Viola herself. And this was the girl whom the world called wild! Here in the kitchen, the heart of the home, was the *real* Viola Lake, the true homebody.

Just the same, I thought it the part of prudence that Viola's chaperon should be included in our social evening, so Viola called through the dumbwaiter for her aunt to descend.

But when Miss Kinko entered, she was accompanied by a friendly escort with whom she planned to dine at a cafeteria and attend the movies. Feeling that her chaperonage was essential, I spoke up. 'Viola,' said I, 'that isn't exactly a good idea!' Viola agreed readily but misunderstanding my inference, remarked to her aunt that ladies didn't go out on social engagements with a sanitary engineer.

So Aunt Minnie, peevish and grumbling, sent her escort on his way and we sat down to dinner. The food was so delicious that this thought flicked through my mind: actually Viola was born to be a cook.

Aunt Minnie's attitude, however, interfered with the spirit of the meal. She was in deep despondency over missing the movies, for it was no ordinary evening but a world première at Grauman's Million-Dollar Theatre.

I finally felt impelled to give Miss Kinko a good lecture. Her place was by Viola's side, I told her, especially at a time when her niece was perilously involved in the Barco trial. However, during the lecture, it crossed my mind that Miss Kinko was paying little, if any, attention; and later, while Vi and I were absorbed in washing dishes, she sneaked out of the house. For some little while we dawdled over the dishes and did not note Aunt Minnie's absence—fortunately for our peace of mind.

It was only later that we learned what Miss Kinko had been up to, and even now the contretemps still causes me to shudder.

It seems that the irresponsible little lady had gone off to the première where she elbowed her way into the front line of the mob waiting outside the theatre. It was

In the kitchen was the real Viola Lake, the true homebody. And this was the girl whom the world called wild.

indeed a night of nights! And to Auntie Minnie, how different from Manitoba! She stood watching in gaping delight as famous film personalities arrived in their multicoloured limousines and descended into the concentrated illumination of fifty army searchlights.

At the entrance of the theatre hung the microphone through which the historic event was being broadcast to the widespread Radio Public. The master of ceremonies was Walter Catlett, a very privileged wit, who was allowed freely to crack jokes at the expense of world-famous folk.

Alice White's car made its way through the howling mob, stopped, and the little star descended, accompanied by her best beau for the evening. Cheers racked Hollywood Boulevard.

'Folks,' called Catlett into the microphone, 'here comes little Alice White with that *great fellow*, Sid Bartlett! When better men are made, Alice will make them, won't you, honey?'

Little Miss White smiled indulgently, stepped to the microphone and spoke. 'I am charmed to be with all of you in spirit on this lovely evening.'

Auntie Minnie was in Heaven. Moreover, she began to sense that she herself was a part of all this! To bystanders right and left, she announced that *she* was the aunt of Viola Lake; in fact, it wasn't long before Miss Kinko had a little fan gallery of her own.

The next auto to attain the entrance was the red underslung sportster of $am (for so he always writes his name) Hardy, that prince of good actors. His little Scottie dog accompanied him. Catlett announced over the phone that $am was accompanied by his 'sweetheart.'

And then, listeners on the *qui vive* to learn who $am's sweetheart might be, had the amusing experience of hearing a bark as $am held his pet to the microphone.

The incident gave Auntie Minnie a daring inspiration! If $am Hardy's dog could be given radio time, merely to bark, why couldn't Viola Lake's aunt say a word or two? She crashed her way through to Catlett and told him who she was. Unluckily (as it turned out afterwards) a delay had developed in the proceedings, when a woman who jumped on the running board of Gary Cooper's car had tossed her arms about his neck and then swooned from excess of emotion.

Catlett, delighted to fit Auntie Minnie into the pause created by the above incident, proceeded to do the honours for Aunt Minnie.

'Folks,' announced Catlett, 'who do you think is right here in this *very lobby?* None other than Viola Lake's aunt, Miss Minola Kinko. Minola—take the mike!'

As, quivering with excitement, Aunt Minnie stepped to the microphone, the Goldmark limousine was drawing up and Goldmark was now fated to hear Auntie Minnie proclaim: 'Ladies and gentlemen, I'm Viola Lake's Auntie Minnie from Manitoba. Viola didn't come tonight because she's getting *her* kicks by staying home with Elmer Bliss!'

'Stop her!' Goldmark yelled over the heads of the crowd, but he wasn't heard.

Proving to be Viola's Nemesis and a born microphone 'hog' to boot, Aunt Minnie went on: 'Seeing that the two of 'em are so sweet on each other, I thought I'd sneak off and leave 'em alone. You know the old adage, two's company and three's a…'

By this time Goldmark had reached Aunt Minnie and throttled her, while she, not knowing Goldmark's motivation, started to yell for help. But Mr Cooper was now pushed through to the microphone and Aunt Minnie, although screaming at the top of her voice that she was being manhandled, had lost the audience's attention. Such is the fragile fabric of human fame!

Well, during the time that Viola and I were thus being involved in scandalous implications over a nationwide radio hookup, we were engaged in nothing more evil than looking over her library. I was amazed at finding any number of books there.

'Viola,' I said earnestly, '*this* is where you belong. Why have you allowed yourself to be led away from it?'

'Because, Elmer,' she answered, 'you are the only man I ever met who ever tried to get me into a library!'

Tears were welling into her eyes as she spoke, and I couldn't resist an impulse to take her little hand. But the tender mood of the moment was violated by a harsh ringing of the door bell. It was Goldmark, accompanied by Aunt Minnie, whom he shoved into the house, at the same time telling us at the top of his voice, about her outrageous broadcast.

I went cold all over! More material for scandal in the Barco case! The Czarship itself involved! I had been put in charge to enforce purity and now an evil-minded world was to say the worst of me! My own spotless reputation sullied!

Goldmark proceeded to issue an ultimatum. Aunt Minnie was to be returned at once to Manitoba. Shaking with sobs, she ran upstairs. Goldmark crisply accepted Viola's apologies for her aunt, and then, clutching me rudely by the hand, he said: 'Come on, young fellow. I'm going to get you back to your Mama!'

But even as Goldmark was driving me home, I began to sense that wild horses couldn't keep me from returning that night to Viola.

We reached the house and Goldmark before departing, personally shoved me through our front doorway in order to make sure that I was safely in my haven. As I stood there on the porch I heard Mother call out from my bedroom where, as usual, she was waiting up for me: 'Is that you, Elmer?'

'Yes, Mother,' I answered. And then, concocting an alibi which would facilitate my return to Viola without being detected, I continued: 'It's a hot night, Mother. I think I'll sleep in the hammock out on the porch.'

'Alrighty Elmer,' came her unsuspicious reply. ('Good,' thought I, 'she hasn't been listening to the radio.') 'I'm bringing you some chocolate cake and a glass of milk, dear.'

'Thank you, Mother,' answered I, and she presently joined me on the porch with her little collation.

We kissed each other good night and then seeing me start as if to remove my jacket, she disappeared into the house. With pulse atingle, I waited until I saw the lights go out in Mother's room. Then, carrying my shoes in hand, I quietly tipped down the front steps. And, in order to keep Mother from hearing the noise of my motor, I had to push my sportster halfway down the hill.

It was dawn before I returned—fatigued, but infinitely exhilarated. I had to push my sportster all the way up the hill, so that Mother would not hear my engine puffing. Then, too exhausted to again take off my clothes, I fell into the hammock. But I was hungry too. For I had not wanted to ask Viola to get up and give me a snack, after she had already prepared so generous a dinner. I reached over to take the chocolate cake and fairly wolfed it down. It seemed, as I did so, that Mother must have used some strange, new, exotic flavouring when she baked it. But not until the next morning did I realize that I must have eaten myriads of red ants with which the residue of cake-crumbs still was swarming.

Well, never mind! It was merely an anticlimax to a night during which the old Elmer Bliss had departed

That night the old Elmer Bliss had departed for ever, replaced by a new Man.

for ever. The smug, narrow-minded Elmer who had evaded life and considered himself *strong* for doing so, was dead and buried. Now a feeling of a broader humanity surged through me. A new understanding of human problems filled my being, a strength to face *any* trial, *any* attack of *any* enemy, not as a bloodless Moralist, but as a vital human being!

'*Viola shall not fall!*' I repeated to the new Elmer Bliss, as I watched the pink light of dawning day. 'I'm a *Man*—and I will save her!'

Nine

Very Naughty Figs

As THE CLIMAX of the Barco trial drew nigh, I found
how strong was the new humanity which gripped me.
Up to that time I had felt, with everyone else, that Barco
must pay the supreme penalty; for murder needed
strong discouragement in Hollywood. But from Viola I
had learned things that I never found in books. I learned
the existence of an urge more powerful than the rules of
safe conduct I had so smugly laid down for myself.

At first the discovery had left me dazed. And then a
broader comprehension of every human deed engulfed
me. I began truly to understand my fellow creatures,
and with understanding came love for one and all of
them. I began to sympathize with the man Barco. I
myself had succumbed to an invincible necessity when
first I took Viola in my arms. The necessity, in his case,
was to kill.

I came out in my column against the death penalty
for Barco.

Now, the unspoken slogan of District Attorney
Welch was: 'Death for Barco; ruin for Viola Lake; the
mayorship of Los Angeles for me!' If Barco escaped the
death penalty, it would upset Welch's political future.

So now Welch and I became more bitter enemies than we had been before. Our antagonism had reached fever heat on the morning Viola was to be called to the witness stand.

By nine o'clock the corridors were jammed. Only a modicum of the crowd could ever hope to get into the courtroom itself, but motherly old ladies and fresh-faced girls were fighting like veritable fiends to break through that doorway and witness a sister soul being led to the slaughter.

Inside the court, the atmosphere was tense. As I made my way to the Czar's chair, I could sense a wave of that perverse psychology which grips a mob when it can begin to destroy a once-loved idol of its own making.

Viola arrived at length, frightened and pale. She was accompanied by a paid companion who had been specially chosen from the Pilgrim Mother files at Central Casting; for at that moment Viola hadn't a single associate whose presence was acceptable to Mrs Grundy.

Presently I noted a solid wedge of determined womanhood milling its way into court, led by Mrs Sarah Allwyn-Krantz, president of the United Women's Clubs of Southern California. One could ascertain from their faces that they were all 'good' women. They had come to hear Viola's testimony and decide whether or not they would demand that Goldmark withdraw her films from circulation. Looking at them I was forced to ask myself what chance Viola had for mercy from any of their ilk?

Now Judge Olah rapped for order. The electric current which suffused the room condensed and intensified. District Attorney Welch arose, and with a studied casualness, addressed the court. 'Your honour,' he said, 'I understand that the murderer's fourth victim, Mrs Belle Geiger, some time previous to her murder, was employed as cook in the home of Viola Lake.'

A tremor ran through the crowd. Although Viola and I had been admonished never to look at each other in public, I noted out of the corner of my eye that she stiffened and took a breath. Then, as in a dream, I heard a seemingly far-off voice say: 'Miss Viola Lake will please take the stand.'

Viola stood up. She looked so weak and frail that I ventured to toss her one short, quick glance of encouragement. Biting a trembling lip, she made her way to the witness stand and in barely audible tones took the oath to speak the truth, the whole truth, and nothing but the truth.

Welch faced her, looking quiet, cold, and even more than usually impersonal.

'Miss Lake, where were you on the night of August 26, 1928?'

It was a trap. Viola knew it, though she had no choice but to enter in. 'I don't remember,' she said, so weakly that one only understood the words from the movement of her lips.

Welch was quick to follow up his advantage. 'Oh, you don't remember?' he said. 'In that case, I have something here which may assist your recollection.' He turned to his assistant at a nearby table. 'Give me that book, please,' he said: 'the diary.'

As the volume was passed to Welch, a tremor ran through the crowd.

Welch stood a moment thumbing through the pages. The crowd leaned forward.

Viola blanched. I scarcely breathed.

At length Welch spoke. 'Miss Lake,' he said, 'this diary was kept by your cook, who seems to have made a comprehensive record of your activities during the time you employed her.'

Viola gripped her chair and took another breath. Her attorney jumped to his feet.

'I object!' he thundered.

Welch, raising his eyebrows in mock surprise, faced Judge Olah for a decision.

Viola's lawyer continued: 'I do not see what possible connection Miss Lake's private actions can have with the murder of this woman.'

Welch smiled superciliously. 'Your Honour,' he said, 'the murderer's lawyers have indicated that Barco killed in self-defence. We've got to know enough of this victim's character to determine the likelihood of such a statement being true. We have no witness so revealing as her diary.'

Judge Olah considered a moment, not wishing to be unfair, and then came the dread decision: 'You may continue.'

The crowd settled back in pleasurable anticipation as Welch, scarcely deigning to smother a smile of triumph, sought for a particular item he had marked. He began to read the account of an episode that had transpired in a New York hotel suite occupied by Viola and the Geiger woman while en route to Hollywood from London. It related that on a certain night, Viola had knocked on the door of the room occupied by Mrs Geiger, waking her from a sound sleep. Viola had then announced that one of Hollywood's Wall Street backers had just arrived in her salon; whereupon she requested Mrs Geiger to provide asylum for another acquaintance who was visiting Viola's boudoir. Mrs Geiger had uncooperatively refused, telling Viola to hide the excess visitor in her clothes basket. But it so happened that he was a member of the orchestra at the Roxy Theatre and the closet wasn't sufficiently roomy for his bass viol.

The crowd tittered. Welch glanced up from the book. 'No one would laugh at Miss Lake's predicament,' he admonished them sarcastically, 'who has ever been called on to hide a bass viol.'

Again Viola's lawyer jumped to his feet. 'Your Honour,' he cried, 'I object! This testimony is incompetent, irrelevant, immaterial, and in no way germane to the issues of this case!'

Welch, a glint of evil lighting up his eye, turned to Olah. 'Your Honour,' he remarked quietly, 'the murderer's lawyers have indicated that this fourth victim possessed a violent temper. We've got to know her reactions under conditions which aroused her ire. These incidents will tell!'

Judge Olah hesitated. Viola went paler. I could have killed Welch with my own two bare fists!

'You may continue,' Olah said.

Still seemingly impersonal, Welch went on. 'Miss Lake,' he asked, 'do you remember a quarrel which took place between you and your cook in October, 1928?'

'I don't remember,' she whispered.

Again Welch fingered the pages of the diary. Again the crowd leaned forward. 'Perhaps this will assist your recollection,' he said brightly.

He read. It was an account of an altercation between Viola and her cook at a time when the woman had objected to preparing breakfast for Viola and a friend.

'I object!' her attorney again roared.

Welch again faced the judge. 'Your Honour,' he said, 'I am only trying to prove that the murderer's victim was *not* possessed of a violent temper. I consider that on this occasion her remonstrances were mild, considering the fact that breakfast was ordered for 6 a.m. because Miss Lake's guest had to get to an early train to meet his wife.'

Jeering laughter. Catcalls were beginning to rise from the back of the room. Judge Olah rapped for order, but it had no effect.

I glanced at Goldmark. His gaze on Mrs Allwyn-Krantz, he looked like a grey ghost, for she was already considering how best to frame the resolution which meant the end of Viola's career.

However, I had had enough! After all, I was Czar! And even if it meant my downfall, I decided to intervene. I jumped to my feet.

'As Czar of this case and in fairness to this young woman, I demand to be heard!' I cried.

Judge Olah rapped sharply. 'Mr Bliss, you are out of order,' he declared.

Then Welch stepped forward, raised his hand, and the crowd, which by this time was with him to the last man, came to attention.

'Your Honour,' said Welch, 'I should like to hear Mr Bliss's excuses for this young woman whom we allow to play a large part in directing the cultural lives of the public. And it has been established by a recent nationwide radio broadcast that his relations with her are intimate enough to make him an authority on the subject.'

More catcalls, more hisses. Some vulgarian called out in derision: 'Elmer loves Vi,' and the crowd hooted. I felt my face go red.

Again Welch raised his hand for silence. 'Mr Bliss has been appointed moral arbiter of this case,' he went

*I had had enough! 'In fairness to this young woman,
I demand to be heard!' I cried.*

on. 'Let him give us an account of *his* activities with the witness since he has been in office!'

'Hear! Hear!' shouted the mob.

I glanced inquiringly toward Judge Olah. He nodded for me to go on!

I stepped to the platform. There were hisses and several 'Boos,' before the crowd settled back into a derisive silence.

'Ladies and gentlemen,' I began, 'you, of your own free will, have raised Viola Lake to be an idol of the great film world. And why have you done this?' I asked. I paused; then answered my own question: 'Because Viola is adorable!'

'You should know!' someone called out. The crowd laughed. It was irritating, but with so much at stake I dared not lose my poise. On I went.

'You chose Viola Lake for stardom because she is temperamental, impetuous, and full of fire. But, suppose she had been carefully balanced, scheming, and cold. Could she ever have scaled the heights of comedy or delved into the depths of pathos for your delight?'

I allowed a moment for this to sink in. 'Mr Welch has just now, with his usual gallantry, brought out the fact that men have fallen in love with Viola Lake. But Mr Welch has mentioned only a few. I could tell you of thousands upon thousands more. I have looked through Miss Lake's fan mail and can attest that a whole world of men is as ready to make love to Viola Lake as those of us who have been lucky enough to have had the opportunity. As I have myself, if you want the truth! Now, in all justice, can you blame me for that?'

I could sense that my frankness had had a certain effect. Perhaps it did no harm to let them know a Czar is a human creature with red blood flowing in his veins!

'Mr Welch,' said I, 'has let you know that Viola Lake listens with compassion to the pleas of men who adore her. But, my friends, would you want Viola to remain untouched and hard of heart, with no sympathy for a fellow being's struggle for attainment?'

This was met by silence, but I could sense that I had startled that unruly mass into thought.

'Ladies and gentlemen,' I said, 'if you take the advice of Mr Welch, you will say to Viola Lake: "Be gay—but mind you hold your gaiety in check; be beautiful—but mind you don't allow yourself to be admired; be glamorous, but mind you never let your glamour cast a spell; and if your nerves are worn to shreds by hours of weary, grilling effort to bring a little of your magic into the drab dullness of our lives, mind you don't allow yourself the relaxation commensurate with your toil. No! No! Go home! And go to bed! And read a book!"'

Someone cried out: 'Elmer's got something there, folks.' Inwardly blessing the man, I was quick to follow my advantage.

'Ladies and gentlemen, if you want to listen to Mr Welch, then I suggest you allow *him* to choose your screen stars in the future—to choose those who are cool-headed, practical, and beyond reproach.

'And if Mr Welch is at a loss to find candidates who possess these homely virtues, I beg to suggest for his approval Prudence Penny, Beatrice Fairfax, and Carrie Chapman Catt!'

The crowd broke into a laugh, and this time the

laugh was on Welch. He flushed and looked furious. But, alas, others in that auditorium were with him in spirit. I could see that Sarah Allwyn-Krantz and her cohorts were still bridling. Something of the cunning of a Machiavelli now gripped me as I faced that group of frustrated womanhood.

'I appeal to you, Mrs Allwyn-Krantz,' I begged, 'to you who, early in life, chose to devote your beauty, grace, and feminine charm to the one purpose of making Mr Allwyn-Krantz happy.'

Mrs Allwyn-Krantz picked up interest. 'Girls,' I heard her murmur, 'maybe we better think things over.'

My strategy was paying dividends! Welch could no longer contain himself. Furious, he leaped at the Allwyn-Krantz woman.

'Don't be duped by this common spellbinder's defence of that creature,' he cried. He shook the diary in her face. 'Why,' he thundered, 'I have it here in black and white that Viola Lake is a drug addict.'

A sudden hush descended on the court.

Judge Olah, to whom this statement was a bombshell, dropped his gavel and leaped to his feet. I looked at Viola. She had gone dead white and looked more frail than ever.

Sneeringly Welch continued. 'This vitality, this personality, this emotional verve Mr Bliss has asked you to admire in his girl-friend, is not the result of artistic temperament, but of artificial stimulation!'

A buzz like a poisonous and audible miasma rose from the crowd.

Viola rose, cast one look of agonized appeal at me, and then slipped to the floor—inert. She had fainted! I did not go to her. Holding myself in check, I was rallying my forces.

Two friendly gentlemen jumped from the front row and started to pick Viola up. 'STOP!' I cried. 'Leave her where she is!'

Something in my tone silenced the entire room. I gestured to Viola's inert figure. 'Look at that broken little creature, my friends. If Viola Lake *were* dependent on drugs for stimulation, would she not have availed herself of them on *this* of all days—knowing she was to be the victim of a brutal attack by Mr Welch.'

'Yes, yes!' spoke up a friendly voice.

'You are intelligent, my friends! Does Viola Lake look as if she has been strengthened by drugs in order to attain the "vitality" and "emotional verve" to which Mr Welch has so sneeringly alluded?'

The crowd stirred. I turned to one of the friendly gentlemen who had leaped to Viola's aid. 'Bring her a glass of California orange juice,' said I. 'Let *it* revive and stimulate her, for it is all she needs!'

At least a dozen eager volunteers rushed to fetch the wholesome libation I suggested, while the crowd broke into applause.

'Bravo! Bravo, Bliss!' they cried.

Losing all control of his temper, Welch pushed forward and shook the diary in the faces of the crowd. 'Will you let me read this!' he screamed. He couldn't even be heard above the catcalls—*catcalls for Welch.* Then, out of the corner of one eye, I noted him with uncontrollable fury, toss the Geiger diary into a waste basket (from which I retrieved it at the end of the session).

As Judge Olah finally succeeded in establishing quiet, I noted Goldmark moving to the fore. 'I think three cheers for Viola ought to be the next thing in the order of court procedure,' he ventured.

Beaming, Olah agreed, and they were given lustily. Tears of emotion welled into Goldmark's eyes as, gesturing to where Viola was now being revived by friendly ministrations, he addressed the court.

'Folks,' said he, 'I want you to know I got Viola under contract for the next five years! And since it's been made public how many emotions she's got, I'm going to let her run more of a gamut than she's ever run before.'

Applause greeted Goldmark's statement. 'But in order to prove that crime don't pay,' he went on, addressing Mrs Allwyn–Krantz, 'I'll allow you ladies of the United Clubs of Southern California to pass on every script, and make sure Viola always winds up behind the eight ball.'

Goldmark's offer broke down the last barrier to Viola's complete and unanimous vindication. Mrs Allwyn–Krantz rose and graciously accepted the assignment in the name of the U.W.C.S.C.

Court was now adjourned for the luncheon hour, a luncheon at which I was able, at last, to appear with Viola in public. I joined her where she stood, the centre of a public which was now stripping her garments of souvenirs and clamouring for autographs; as they also proceeded to do in the case of my humble self. And while I was trying to cope with their demands from right and left, I thought I heard a voice call out: 'Why not Bliss for mayor of Los Angeles?'

My heart stood still. Had I heard aright? Yes! The cry

was taken up and carried on: 'Bliss for mayor!' I looked at Welch and saw him wince.

At length, after the tumult and the shouting finally died, I was leading Viola from court when we happened upon Welch in the corridor.

'Congratulations, Bliss!' he said derisively. 'You've made them swallow nearly every crime in the moral calendar! But mark my words, your championship of Barco is going to be your downfall!'

'Ah, yes?' I asked.

'This town will never countenance a mayor who urges that the murderer of seven helpless women should go free.'

He sneered and strode away. But I had scarcely heard him, for my thoughts were on the heights. Why shouldn't I save Barco, as I had saved Viola; attain the mayorship from a platform based on Love for all Humanity? What could be more in harmony with Los Angeles, our 'City of the Angels'?

Ten

Viola Vindicated

NOW WAS THE trial nearing its crux. I had every confidence of saving Barco's life, for it was obvious to me that none of God's creatures, in his right mind, could murder seven women. So I had suggested insanity as the grounds for his acquittal. But, as it turned out, Barco was to give me less than no assistance.

A stubborn old codger, he was possessed of an absurd egotism. Neither his lawyers nor I could get Barco to admit to mental lapses of any sort. When we tried to make him remember his sensations prior to the murders, he became wildly antagonistic.

'I know what you're trying to do!' he would exclaim. 'You're trying to get evidence that I'm not right in the head. But let me tell you, none of us Barcos has ever been in an asylum yet, and I'm not going to be the first to bring disgrace on the family.'

When the day finally arrived for Barco to mount the witness stand I had become no end perturbed. I visualized the poor man playing directly into the hands of Welch who sneeringly insisted that he was as sane as any of us; and that Southern California should start a 'house-cleaning campaign' by sending him to the gallows.

In court that morning were representatives from papers all over the country, for Barco's account of his own murders was to be news of the first rank.

C. C. Cahoon and the boys from the Chamber of Commerce were present to root for me, while Welch also had his adherents, foremost of whom, of course, was Lansing Marshall. However, the main body of boosters for Southern California were behind me to a man.

Barco mounted the witness stand. His first testimony took the form of outlining history previous to arrival in the Golden State. He informed the court that he had been a resident of Duluth, where he had held the position of watchman in the public library. Barco stated that, sitting in the furnace room of the library at night, he had done a great deal of reading, primarily of the Bible, but also of nature books and poetry. And he had formed an overpowering impulse to go to Southern California and live out his days in that Paradise on earth, where life would be a foretaste of the everlasting Heaven beyond. He described how he had scraped together sufficient money for the trip and had finally arrived at his long-dreamed-of goal.

Barco then told how he had been overcome by finding Nature here at its apotheosis. In Duluth, he had had to satisfy a craving for growing things by keeping a few meagre geraniums in pots on a window sill, while here he lived in a veritable bower of luxuriant foliage, fruits, and flowers.

There in Duluth, Barco had longed for pets, but felt

it cruel to keep the little things in the furnace room of the library. Here in California, he had all the chickens and rabbits for which a man could wish; he had given them nicknames and made pets of them.

He stated that in Duluth he had not always been able to buy everything the market afforded in food, while out here the fruits of tree and earth and bush fell into his lap for almost nothing—gifts from Mother Nature who showers them without stint on her children who live in this blessed spot. Barco stated that Nature in Southern California seemed to him to be God's presence here on earth.

I must say that at this point in Barco's testimony I began to worry. For his statements were obviously true and certainly bespoke a sane and healthy mind. Could I be wrong in my contention that he was a maniac?

I looked at the jury. They were leaning forward, drinking in every word with interest and approval.

'And then,' continued Barco, 'it began to dawn on me that things were happening here in the Southland that I'd never read of in the poetry books. *And I began to have my doubt about the Divine Presence in Nature.* Back in Duluth,' he said, 'my little potted geraniums had to put up a struggle just to live. But out here, the same kind of geraniums ran riot and grew so fast I could hardly believe my eyes! Then I began to notice that those geraniums had no compassion on the other little green things that tried to grow beside 'em. They choked to death every other plant that got in their way. And I began to wonder if Nature unrestrained is such a noble institution, after all.

'And then,' Barco went on, 'it began to dawn on me

that ruthless destruction was rampant all around me. Scarcely a week went by, that coyotes didn't get in and kill one of my rabbits or a chicken. And I began to understand that Nature is nothing but one long, relentless fight for the survival of *brute strength*.

'The laws of Nature break every single precept of the Christian religion, which teaches kindness, humility, and sacrifice. I'm telling you,' he vituperated, his voice aquiver with passion, 'Nature is the Antichrist!

'Yes,' screamed Barco, 'Southern California, where Nature runs rampant, is nothing but the Devil's Playground!'

I looked at the jury. They sat there stunned, listening to Barco as if he were revealing to them a whole new field of thought.

'And then,' he went on, 'I began to notice the effect this place had on my fellow beings. I found them all wallowing in creature comforts which come from being warmed by constant sunshine and glutted by the Devil's abundant fruits—the eyes of men ravished by beautiful girls. I began to grow hungry for spiritual food, so I joined all the religious cults, one after the other. But I found every one of them was sodden with Nature worship which is nothing but the worship of the Devil and the body.'

The old fellow now reached into the bosom of his sport shirt and drew forth a well-thumbed Bible.

'I'm going to read to you from Jeremiah—chapter twenty-four—verses one and two.' He opened to the passage and in sonorous, Biblical tones, proceeded to intone: 'The Lord showed me and behold two baskets of figs were set before the temple. One basket had very good figs, even like the figs that are first ripe; and the other basket had very naughty figs, which could not be eaten, they were so bad. Then said the Lord unto me: "What seest thou, Jeremiah?" And I said "Figs…the good figs are very good, and the evil, that cannot be eaten, they are so evil."'

Closing his Bible, he shook it in our faces. 'And I'm telling you, the women I picked up on Hollywood Boulevard were the worst of the lot. They were old and ugly and beat-up; they were the kind that, back in Duluth, would have had their minds on higher things. But out here? Oh, no! Southern California had given them one idea; to catch up with all the hankey-pankey they'd missed out on in Duluth.

'Oh, I started off by doing right by 'em! I married 'em! And then I tried to save their souls. But did they want to be saved ? They did not! They wanted to go right on bleaching their hair and painting their faces and trying to get *me* to fall from grace. So I saved them the only way I knew. I killed them all dead!

'But I got 'em away from the temptations and flesh pots of this anteroom to hell,' he roared. 'And anyone who claims I'm insane only shows his ignorance of what goes on in this Paradise of physical gratifications, spiritual sunstroke, mental stagnation, and flimsy morals!'

(Now he was quoting Lansing Marshall!)

Barco sat down. You could have heard a pin drop. We were too stunned, all of us, to make a move.

With the smile of the cat that has swallowed the canary, Welch arose to sum up.

'You have all heard Barco,' he said, 'and you know now that the man is of course, absolutely sane. For years

I have been crying from the housetops that we of Southern California need to put up a very special fight against moral laxness.

'We are still, in a certain sense, a pioneer community. We are constantly drawing flotsam and jetsam in large numbers from every quarter of the globe; people who come here to ply illegal trades of every sort. And what are we *good* citizens doing about it?

'We good citizens are lolling in the sun, playing golf, developing a dangerous complacency and a spirit of *dolce far niente* which make us helpless against the inroads of all sorts of shoddy institutions. Hollywood has become a byword throughout the entire civilized world for everything that's tawdry and immoral!'

(Now he, too, was quoting Marshall.)

For a painful half-hour Welch continued in this vein and ended with a final appeal to the jury for the death penalty.

'I demand death for Barco,' he cried, 'because as a sane man he must pay the penalty of the law! But I ask that his sacrifice be not in vain, and that his words of wisdom will prompt us all to face the situation here like men. I thank you.'

It was now time for adjournment. But we of the booster contingent felt impelled to meet in Olah's private chambers for a consultation. So I kissed Viola good-bye, and after admonishing her to go home and take a nap, we parted.

Assembling in the judge's chamber, C. C. was the first to voice his consternation. 'This is awful!' he said. 'If the jury declares Barco sane it will discredit every bit of propaganda the Chamber of Commerce has sent out

132

for years. And at a moment when the winter tourist season is approaching its zenith.'

'C. C.'s right,' spoke up Milton Purdy. 'What will happen when prospective tourists read in tomorrow's papers Barco's contention that California is the Devil's Playground?'

The thought was shattering. But what to do? We were so stunned, all of us, that no ideas came. At length we decided to go home and think, and meet again next morning.

On the way to our hilltop, dark thoughts of doubt began to assail me. Could Barco, Welch, and even Lansing Marshall possibly be right? Had I myself fallen into a trap? Should I, perhaps, renounce Viola? This was a thought I quickly banished, knowing such a sacrifice to be beyond my strength. But just the same, my Paradise had been invaded.

I arrived home and told Mother what had happened at the trial. From her I got no sympathy. Mother had long since washed her hands of what she termed 'the whole nasty mess.'

'You should have known no good could come of your trying to save the life of that murderer. You're not the Elmer I gave birth to! And what's more, you never will be, until you give up that dope fiend!'

Had Mother been more of a comfort that afternoon, I might have remained home for a while. But I knew of someone else who could assuage my loneliness and my doubts.

I hastened to Viola. She was away from the house when I arrived there, but sensing that I might seek her out, she had left me a note.

'Dear Cookie-Face,' it read, 'I've gone over to Lansing Marshall's apartment to see if I can get him to lay off you for a change. I'll be back in a bang. I love you. Vi.'

Her thoughtful errand to Marshall on my behalf assuaged my last doubts as to the advisability of our union, when the day came that it could be legalized. My thoughts went even further afield! What a lady-mayoress she might become! What a helpmeet! What an inspiration! Why, bless her heart, she had inspired me already! A thought percolated in my mind, a plan to undo the evil Barco had inflicted on the Southland.

Due that evening for my regular Thursday radio chat over ZWX I went to the phone and called up the station.

'May I change the subject of my radio talk this evening?' I asked.

'Why, certainly,' came the reply.

'Then,' I said, 'I wish you to start announcing every fifteen minutes, up to the time I take the air, that tonight I'm going to give full details of the murders of the archfiend Barco.'

'Wait a minute, Elmer, old boy,' came the amazed rejoinder. 'You know we don't broadcast that sort of stuff.'

'Have I ever yet said anything to offend our listeners?' I asked.

'No,' came the reply. 'But this subject doesn't sound like you, Elmer.'

'That's all right!' I affirmed. 'I want the largest radio audience in America tonight, and you can count on my integrity for the rest.'

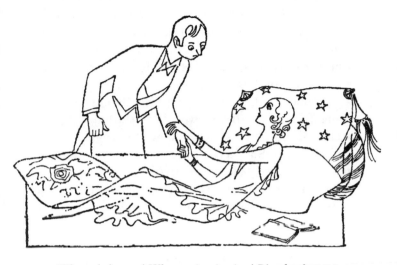

What a helpmeet! What an inspiration! Bless her heart,
she had inspired me already!

Although I sensed that there were qualms, the matter was finally agreed. I then called up C. C. Cahoon.

'I can't stop to talk now, C. C.,' I told him, 'because I've got to work like the devil for the next two hours! But I'm going to save Southern California. Tune in on me at eight and you'll know all about it.'

It was only a few minutes before eight o'clock that my data was in order. I rushed to the station. They told me that inquiries about my broadcast had flooded the switchboard all day, from all over America. Eight o'clock struck and the announcer took the microphone. I myself had penned his introduction.

'Ladies and gentlemen. One of the most sensational

murder trials in the history of Southern California reached a climax today when Cal Barco mounted the witness stand and told his gruesome story. As you all know, the Czar of this case is our own Elmer Bliss, and who better than he can describe to our listeners the grisly details of those atrocities?'

I stepped to the microphone. 'Neighbours and far-flung friends of all the world,' I started out, 'the archfiend and woman-hacker known to ignominy as Cal Barco came to Southern California nine years ago and settled in Beverly Hills...*Beverly Hills*, a town which showed the greatest increase in population in the 1930 census of any community in the United States, outstripping in the miraculous rapidity of its growth New York, Chicago, and Detroit.

'It was while dwelling in Beverly Hills,' I went on, 'that Barco made the acquaintance of one Hazel Markle and induced her to marry and live with him in a tent house. For such is the salubrious climate of Southern California that one may live snugly all year round in canvas! Think of that, you folks who pay exorbitant coal bills in the freezing East.

'The murder of the Markle woman was effected by a hatchet from a set of garden tools. For Barco had become a zealous gardener on learning that the rotation of crops in Southern California is so rapid as to assure an abundant harvest *every four months* throughout the year. I venture that sounds like Paradise to you farmer folk listening in from the wind-swept plains of Kansas.

'Barco placed the body in an old suitcase, and then carefully washed away all traces of the crime with water which, at that time, he had to carry in buckets from an artesian well. Today, an ample supply of crystal-clear water is to be had anywhere in Southern California by the simple turning of a tap.

'Barco put the gruesome suitcase into his car and drove to Santa Monica, a city where for 365 days of the year the world's most shapely girls dip fresh young bodies into the caressing waves of the Pacific!

'Barco could find no spot in Santa Monica to get rid of his bloody burden, for the ocean is solidly built up with the impressive beach homes of our moving-picture folk.

'Discouraged, Barco drove farther along, past Venice-by-the-Sea, that replica of an historic beauty spot of the old world whose spirit we have managed to capture in lath and plaster, to which we have added such modern improvements as scenic railways, "giggle houses," hot-dog and waffle stands, and all the other delights dear to the heart of the holiday makers.

'At length Barco reached the sand dunes beyond Venice. There he buried his loathsome burden, knowing it was safe beneath the unshifting sand. For the beaches of Southern California are not windswept as are those of the East. Out here, "Let's go to the beach" may be suggested just as rationally in December as in July.'

I paused but a moment for breath and then went on through the remaining six atrocities in all their ghastly details, but with the horror softened and sweetened by true data about Southern California.

Finally I reached the end of the story and said a bright farewell.

As I backed away from the microphone, C. C. rushed to throw his arms about me.

'Well, Elmer, you've done it again!' he said, his face aglow with pride.

My broadcast had indeed gone over in a big way—as was later to be proved by the largest influx of tourists our old Southland had ever entertained.

As hastily as good manners permitted, I freed myself from C. C. and the studio staff at ZWX and repaired to Viola's. There I found out that she had not as yet returned from Marshall's. This seemed rather odd. I sat and waited for her; waited an hour. Then I bethought me of phoning Marshall's apartment house. The polite switchboard operator announced that he had departed for the Soviet Union on an assignment. I asked when he had left the apartment.

'About an hour ago,' came the reply.

'Dear Cookie-Face...' Viola wrote.

'How strange,' thought I. 'Viola should be home by now!' Then I waited…waited…waited.

Yes, Viola accompanied Marshall on his trip to Moscow. (And by-the-by, his account of life there, as being only second to that of Hollywood in the realm of the unthinkable, made newspaper history.)

About two months after Viola's disappearance, I received her letter.

'Dear Cookie-Face,' she wrote, 'I only knew one way to make Lansing lay off you, but after it worked, I didn't have the nerve to look you in the eye again. The truth is, I'm not good enough for you, honey.

'So now you've got the lowdown.

'Please kiss Droopy Drawers (alias Ben Goldmark) for me and tell him there's a blonde car-hop at the drive-in on Sunset and Gower who will slip into my roles without even a stutter.[1]

'I'll never forget you, Cookie dear. Goodbye now.

Vi.'

How quickly all those years have passed! And now I'm looking out the window of my newspaper office in Anaheim. I've spent the whole morning resurrecting the past in my mind, thinking…thinking.

I had learned years ago of Viola's return to Hollywood. Fugitives from the cinema invariably drift back, in the hope of reviving their past triumphs. I also knew that Darryl Zanuck had placed her under contract for extra work, as he so generously does in the case of needy screen stars.

[1] Miss Lake's suggestion proved her to be something of a talent scout. Today the car-hop in question is one of Hollywood's top ranking box office draws. *Ed.*

139

It would have taken little effort to look Viola up, for Anaheim and Hollywood are neighbouring cities of our Southland. Why, then, had I chosen *not* to contact her?

Anyone who poses such a question knows little of the deep hurt a man suffers through a repudiation of his favours; a rejection of his masculine authority and guidance.

But time has dulled the pain now, and I mustn't be unfair. Suppose Viola has come to regret her past? Suppose that on her bed of pain she had learned contrition? Should I not grant my fellow creature the chance to ease her mind of guilt; to say, 'Elmer, I'm sorry'?

It took me four hours to drive the short distance between Anaheim and Van Nuys. For I by-passed the death-defying perils of the Freeway, in favour of the bottleneck of city streets. (Small wonder, thought I, that the closest friends so seldom get together in the broad domain called Hollywood.)

As my car crept along, I pondered on the changes of these past thirty years. The advertisements on marquees I passed were largely for pictures filmed in Rome; and the few that *were* shot in Hollywood, how different from those of the old days! There was one particular movie of Alfred Hitchcock, featuring an incestuous relationship between a lad and his grandmother, combined with necrophilia. And there was that certain murder film of Otto Preminger's in which the murderer goes scot free and our fine, clean-cut, upstanding American star, Jimmy Stewart, is required to shrug the whole thing off and make a mock of Justice.

I passed the old Goldmark studio. It has now been taken over by television, and on the self-same stages where Ben Goldmark once sought to demonstrate that crime doesn't pay, they're shooting ruthless Westerns for our sadistic young fry of today.

Viola's English mansion (its thatched roof replaced) is occupied by a toy factory engaged in the manufacture of nuclear bombs for the kiddies.

Most of the quaint architectural spots I once had publicized on post cards have been removed. Giant apartment buildings of glass and steel erupt in their places. Apartment buildings, did I say? No, no! They are de-humanized containers for the human product, a product of which each specimen is just like all the others.

No more does one see Gloria Swansons in Hollywood; there are no more Joan Crawfords. The stars of today consort in supermarkets with Beverly Hills housewives, whom they ape. And today's most 'glamorous' social set boasts of itself as a 'rat pack'.

Ah me, the Hollywood of yester-year! The Hollywood of Doug and Mary, derring-do and saucy curls, the Hollywood of Shirley Temple, Rin-Tin-Tin.

'Childish' is the word with which the intelligentsia once branded Hollywood. And yet, those movies, which depicted Life as life can never be, were fairy tales for the adult. Today there are no fairy tales for us to believe in, and this is possibly a reason for the universal prevalence of mental crack-up. Yes, if we were childish in the past, I wish we could be children once again.

With heart aflutter, I entered the opulent confines of the Motion Picture Country Club. I was shown to

Viola's room. It proved to be a dainty, cheerful chamber. But Viola's bed was of the hospital variety and she lay there rigidly in traction. I found her face unravaged by the years; indeed she hadn't seemed to mature much since the old days; her eyes were merry and her curls still golden. On the other hand, I had to introduce myself, for my hair, much of which had long since departed, is snowy now.

After Viola's first amazement at seeing me again the conversation eased. We talked at length; talked of the old days, of the Barco trial and of the poor man's execution, of our mutual enemy Mayor Welch, of my beloved mother! I described how my loss, after Mother passed on, had filled my waking moments with a haunting pain for many years. Viola ventured her opinion that an aggravating person can be even more regretted than one who has been colourlessly a comfort. And in all fairness I could but agree.

Viola wanted to know if I still, to quote my own words, penned my thoughts.' I told her yes, indeed, but explained how, as time went on, I seemed to belong less and less to the *new* Hollywood; how I had been forced to sever my connection with the *Tidings* and had purchased the Anaheim *Gazette*. Among the Anaheimites my little sheet is regarded as Scripture and they read me as a Prophet.

Before parting from Viola, I opened a way for her to voice her retribution.

Without saying that I contemplated a work on the order of the recent 'confessions' of screen stars which invariably end on a note of contrition, I asked Viola what lesson *she* had learned from the mistakes of her unhappy, misspent life. Viola's expression bespoke puzzlement. I studied her for a hint of the remorse which would provide a theme for my intended opus and absolve my readers of guilt over having enjoyed its horrendous details. Finally her whole face lit up.

'I know, Elmer!' she said. 'If I had it to live over again, I wouldn't bob my hair!'

I left, bewildered and let down by her response. Walking down the murky path, obscured by the smog of these latter days, I searched the innermost crannies of my mind for a glint of the optimism which had never before failed me. Over and over I asked myself, 'What chance for salvation has that poor, unregenerate soul?'

And then the answer came. Viola was still a child, a child of the old Hollywood. A strange elation began to flood my being as I pondered, 'Except ye become as little children, ye shall not enter the kingdom of heaven.'

Tonight, after the late, late, late show, when Anaheim sleeps and all is quiet, I shall sit down to my typewriter and, with my faith in humanity as a theme, I shall pen the story of Viola and the dear, dead Hollywood I knew.